Three to Die

Garry Maine had spent years in the State Pen for the part he had played in the Powder River Mine Robbery but he never revealed the names of the members of the gang. These three were now wealthy, respected citizens and Garry had come for revenge because the others had let him suffer and had cheated him. They would die.

But nothing was as simple as it seemed and Garry, despite being a real fighter and expert gunman, was no killer. The others had no such scruples though and Garry was fortunate indeed to escape a hanging and a dry gulching. Only his determination and lightning draw had kept him alive so far. For how long would his luck last? Could justice ever be done?

Three to Die

WES YANCEY

A Black Horse Western

ROBERT HALE · LONDON

Robert Hale Limited
Clerkenwell House
Clerkenwell Green
London EC1R 0HT

Typeset by
Derek Doyle & Associates, Liverpool.
Printed and bound in Great Britain by
Antony Rowe Limited, Wiltshire

Three to Die

1

The Hanging Man

The man high on the ridge watching the men in the hollow below shook his head, a whimsical smile playing on his lips as he fingered the barrel of his rifle lovingly. Squatting in the long grass, sweet from recent rain in this corner of Montana, he was a dandified figure in a new blue-serge suit and fawn stetson.

Three riders on big sleek chestnuts circled a tall man. He stood with his feet apart, his battered, travel-stained hat pushed back to reveal thick black hair. His gunbelt and saddle lay beside the bedroll, near the fire that glowed redly. The big man, taut with anger, his mouth compressed into a thin line, waited. His red shirt was half open and dark hair showed on his chest.

Behind a tree was his tethered horse, a patient animal that had taken him many miles in the past week.

Garry Maine knew the three sneering men were playing with him. A dive for his gun would send a bullet his way. The three men hated his guts.

'You're not coming to Cedar Springs – or within thirty miles of the town, Maine. In fact, you're not wanted anywhere in the area . . .' The speaker sat his horse, hunched forward, his fleshy face twisted. He wore a checked jacket and a narrow brimmed black hat. There was little about the appearance of this thick-set man to suggest that he owned a big ranch and could buy up all his neighbours if he wished.

The mounted men were about the same age, around the forty-years mark, and all were heavy with good living. The two who accompanied the rancher wore suits, hard-wearing serges somewhat out of shape because of the heavy Colts. The guns hadn't seen much use, but then a lawyer and a saloon owner weren't usually gunhands. They were Caleb Kray, who found legal work far beyond the large, flourishing town of Cedar Springs, and Mick Fulton, whose drinking and gambling den occupied two floors on a big corner site in Cedar Springs. All the same,

Garry Maine knew they could use their weapons, and he was three yards away from his own gun.

'I know you three don't want me around,' Garry said. 'But ain't this still a free country? I mean, who's gonna stop me from ridin' into town?'

'We've stopped you,' said the rancher.

'But you'll have to kill me to stop me permanently . . .'

The rancher scowled. 'Look, Maine, we know you're as big, hard and stubborn as all hell, but we don't want you in our town. You see, we know why you're heading for Cedar Springs, and that's why we're here. You can take a warning and ride off, or we can finish you right now.'

'Let me strap on my gun and then try it, Mr Luke Behan,' Garry said.

'Think we're fools!' the rancher suddenly raged, his anger plus his fear of this man surging to the surface.

It was Caleb Kray who put in the next few words, his lined, hawk-like face tight with distrust. 'You've come all the way from the prison at Butte to kill us, Maine. We knew you were on your way to Cedar Springs three days ago.'

It was Mick Fulton who'd put on the most weight in the past three years, Garry Maine decided; the saloon keeper looked soft and nervous. And he was afraid.

'Look, Maine, maybe you're a bit short of cash, huh?' Mick Fulton said eagerly. He was perspiring. 'We could give you some cash – call it a loan – then you could just ride on, huh? You don't want trouble, Maine – not after you've just done three years.'

Garry Maine smiled. 'You three gents put me in that pen. Your money would come in mighty handy. Let's say ten thousand dollars – handed over tomorrow in town . . .'

Mick Fulton spluttered and his horse began to sidestep restlessly.

Luke Behan swore and said, 'Ten thousand dollars! Hell! You're headin' for a slug, Maine.'

'But if he'd leave us alone —' began Mick Fulton.

The rancher turned on him. 'He'd take the cash and still try to kill us! You're a fool, Mick. No – he's got to die now.'

The fleshy-faced man reached for his Colt and tugged it from the leather. Garry watched, blank-faced.

'Hold it, Luke,' said Caleb Kray, his temper under control, as always. 'I've got a better idea.'

'He's got to die,' raged Luke Behan. 'You know that, Kray. You know why he's here.'

The other nodded and glanced at the large tree behind Garry Maine. 'Hang him,' he said.

'I'm a lawyer and you're a rancher. We can say he was stealing our horses. You know we can make it stick with the sheriff.'

The rancher paused, gun in hand. 'Maybe you're right. Hanging is the only fit end for a horse-thief . . .'

Caleb Kray dismounted and uncoiled the rope from his saddlehorn. 'Cover him, Luke. You, too, Mick.'

The lawyer slung the rope over a strong branch of the tree, then he fashioned a loop with a running knot and smiled at Garry Maine. 'You could make a try for freedom, Maine.'

'Why should I?' said Garry. 'You three are the dead men.'

'You're finished,' said Caleb Kray. 'But you've got a choice. You can run and take a bullet – or you can live another five minutes and hang.'

The lawyer had kicked Garry's gunbelt even farther away. His rifle was leaning against the tree, on the other side. Garry stood silent and tense, conscious that the water in the can on the fire was boiling madly. It was a crazy thought, but right now he should be enjoying his breakfast. He had been careless; they'd horse-circled him in seconds while he'd wondered about the hoofbeats he'd heard.

Two guns were pointed at him. Caleb Kray

walked behind him, making sure he didn't get in the line of fire.

Garry Maine figured he'd make his move when Kray dropped the loop over his head. So he waited for the moment when he'd grab at Caleb Kray's hands or neck. Then the blow fell – a gunbutt descending on his head. He should have known that Caleb Kray would take no chances.

As Garry swayed, not completely unconscious, the rope loop was dropped over his head. The noose tightened. Garry sank to his knees, his brain reeling from the blow. He was hardly aware of it when the rope hauled him back to his feet. He stood on his toes as Caleb Kray swung the end of the rope to Luke Behan.

'Put two turns around your saddlehorn and we'll haul him up good and proper, Luke.'

The rope end was made fast and then the horse was coaxed forward. Garry's feet left the ground and he dangled. Choking, he jerked and twisted. The instinct for survival penetrated the haze in his brain and made him clutch at the rope biting deeply into his neck. But his fingers could do nothing to help him. His mouth gaped and he sucked for air. His legs thrashed at space.

Kray fastened the rope around the tree bole and mounted his horse. The three men sat their saddles to watch this man die. But Mick Fulton suddenly turned his head.

'I'm goin'! I don't want to see this . . .'

Luke Behan sneered back. 'What're you scared of? A dying man? Remember, Mick, he came here to kill us!'

But Mick Fulton jabbed his horse forward and rode down the grassy, tree-studded slope. Caleb Kray was equally as hard as the rancher but he felt the job of disposing of the threat of Garry Maine was over.

'Come on, Luke, let's ride. We've dirtied our hands enough.'

He jigged his animal into a lope. With a muttered curse, Luke Behan sent his horse in the same direction.

Garry Maine didn't hang long enough to die. The man on the ridge came running down, rifle in hand. His stride was long and lithe, the action of a young man. As he reached the swinging body, he whipped out a knife and severed the rope. Garry Maine fell to the earth and lay huddled there, his senses on the borderline of eternal blackness. The stranger bent over him and eased the rope from around his neck, shaking his head at the sight of the rope burn. The man slapped gently at Garry's cheeks and when he saw his eyelids flicker he rose.

'You'll live, Mr Maine,' he muttered, then he went back up the slope, his rifle cradled in his arms.

He sat his horse long enough to watch Garry Maine stagger to his feet. Then he rode down the other side of the ridge and out of sight.

Garry leaned back against the tree, his hands gingerly feeling at his neck. He felt stiffness creeping into the muscles and knew he'd have a painful crick in the neck for some time. He stared around, aware that he was alone. It didn't make sense. They must have left him for dead — but who had cut the rope?

He bent and picked up the rope. There was a clean slice through the strands. A sharp knife had been used. He went back to the tree, picked up his gunbelt and buckled it on. Patting the Colt .45, he knew he had to kill the three men. Not only had they robbed him of a small fortune — they'd left him to rot in a prison. He'd been sentenced to seven years but a few months ago he'd saved the penitentiary governor from an attack by a crazed prisoner and for that he'd earned a remission of sentence.

He saddled his horse, slid the rifle into its scabbard and secured his saddlebags and bedroll. Then he rode off.

He was curious about his missing rescuer and

so he went through the routine of looking for sign. On soft ground he saw hoofprints and concluded they were made by the departing would-be lynchers. Then he circled the ridges on both sides of the wooded valley. But he discovered nothing.

He turned the horse and headed for Cedar Springs.

He knew this area well. Years ago, when he'd been a wild young hellion, he'd become familiar with all the hills and valleys. He knew he was about three hours out from Cedar Springs.

An hour or so later he ate some dry crusts of bread, swallowing carefully and feeling pain in the swollen muscles in his neck. Finally he took a bandanna from his bag and tied it around the deep rope burns and bruises on his neck.

Descending from a wooded ridge he saw a vast valley ahead, and tiny dots that were steers roaming the open land. He could see a large house with pole corrals and barns all around it. A prosperous spread, no doubt. A trail led around the ridge, marked with wheel tracks. Garry took to this clear way, his mind still on the distant town. Then he rounded a thick stand of sycamores and saw a girl savagely whipping an Indian.

She was using a horsewhip as she held the reins

of her horse with her left hand. The Indian cowered, his hands trying to cover his face and head. His white man's shirt was ragged and dirty. His trousers were of Indian origin, handworked buckskin scuffed at the knees. He wore old moccasins. She hit the Indian repeatedly, her temper apparently out of control. She was a tall girl of about twenty, in jeans instead of a divided riding skirt. She had long fair hair that fell around her neck as if wildness was something she liked.

Garry Maine rode his horse down on her, leaned over and snatched the whip from her hand. She jerked back in astonishment, her blue eyes wide.

'Who the devil are you? What do you mean by—'

'I'm doing you a favour,' he said. 'You figure to kill this redskin?'

'He stole things from the ranch.'

'What kind of things?'

'Some money and a knife . . . and some food.'

'Maybe he was hungry,' said Garry. 'The way you've whipped him, he'll have weals on his back for weeks. That shirt ain't much protection, lady.'

She snapped back, 'He's just a low, thieving Indian! The whip is too good for him.'

Garry Maine smiled. 'You sure don't sound like a lady. Now I always figured a girl who wore jeans was just some poor hick from the hills.'

'You damned saddletramp!'

Garry gave a short laugh. 'You don't talk much like a lady either.'

'My father owns that ranch.' She pointed at the distant buildings. 'Give me back my whip.'

'Maybe you'd like to try it on me.' He flung the whip into a nearby thicket and looked at the Indian. Blood stained his shirt. Garry turned to the girl. 'Maybe you should try apologising to this Injun.'

'Apologise!' She nearly screamed in her anger. 'Go to hell!'

'You even swear like a man.'

Furiously, she reached out and grabbed at his boot, then she pulled, trying to unsaddle him. But he merely leaned his weight towards her and jigged his horse around.

'You big nothing!' she cried. 'Get off this land. It belongs to the T Bar T. You're trespassing. I'll get my father and his men to sling you out like a dead coyote.'

Something jagged at his memory. 'The T Bar T. That's owned by a man called Behan. He bought it three years ago.'

'My father.'

He leaned on the saddlehorn. 'I didn't know Luke Behan was married.'

'He's my stepfather,' she said. 'My mother married him when he took over this ranch. He's hard but he treats me fair.' She gave a sound of irritation. 'Why the devil I should carry on a conversation with a no-account drifter like you I don't know. I just warn you, mister – get before I find a cowhand to drag you off this land on the end of a lariat.'

'I've had enough of rope,' he said. 'I'll go.'

He rode off, tall in the saddle, a big man on a big black stallion. Despite her anger, she wondered who he was.

2

One is a Coward

Garry Maine tied his horse outside a neat white house that bore a shingle with the words: *Doctor Saville. No animals*. He saw the doctor, had some ointment rubbed into his rope burns and parted with a silver dollar. He then took his horse to the livery and ordered oats for him; the stallion needed a change from grass.

Garry slept that night in a hotel room after a big steak and several whiskies. But before sleep came he thought about the three men who'd cost him three years of his life and had then tried to hang him.

He would get it over with; kill them singly, one after the other, and then ride out.

A few scraps of information had come to him through the prison grapevine He'd learned that

Luke Behan had bought a ranch called the T Bar T with his share of the loot, but he hadn't known that the man had married. He'd also got to know that Caleb Kray had built up a good law practice in Cedar Springs. The lawyer was rich now. And Mick Fulton, once a cheap thief, was now the owner of a big saloon and gambling house where some of the wealthiest men in the county gathered to play poker and roulette.

Garry Maine stirred in his sleep. How could he rest knowing these three men had bested him? Three tricky rogues who'd fooled him completely! He'd taken the rap and they had collected the gold. The details – well, he knew the details now by heart. He'd jog their memories just before he killed them. He awakened at ten that night and went along the boardwalk. He'd heard all about Mick Fulton's place when in jail. It was called the Gold Cougar, an apt name. The place was the biggest in town – and Cedar Springs had five saloons apart from first-class hotels and two tent outfits down by the river rapids.

Two men glanced at Garry as he passed. His sheepskin coat was buttoned up, for the night air was cool. Garry went down the main street, came to a corner and looked around. Street lights burned. Horses plodded down the hard-baked road. Light spilled from one saloon. He looked up at the false front; it wasn't the Gold Cougar.

Garry soon found the place. Many horses stood at the tierail and a pair of wagons were parked. Lights blazed from all windows in the big building. Over the entrance was a painted sign showing a stalking cougar.

Garry walked into the crowded saloon. A piano tinkled a fast tune. He was curious about this place Mick had acquired three years ago.

After Garry Maine went through the batwings a man stopped just behind him on the boardwalk. The man smiled. His blue-serge suit and new fawn stetson had been brushed free of travel dust. He did not, however, carry a rifle. But he was not weaponless. Cedar Springs was getting bigger every day, but the day of the gun had not passed. Under the man's long jacket was a leather gunbelt, and in the holster was a staghorn-butted Colt Peacemaker.

Over the batwings he watched Garry Maine move up to the bar counter and look around. He thought the big man looked healthy for a fellow who'd dangled at the end of a rope only that afternoon.

The saloon room was typical of drinking places in frontier towns. Men stood around and argued about cattle and timber. Saloon girls favoured a certain few with their attentions.

Garry Maine came to the conclusion that Mick Fulton would be somewhere on the first floor, maybe at the card tables where money was being thrown around.

Suddenly incensed with hatred for the three men who were now well-to-do while he still bore the mental scars of three years under brutal warders, he headed for a winding stair-case that climbed one wall. Maybe he would find Mick Fulton and scare the hell out of the man. Why not? Why wait? Maybe he'd kill the tricky bastard right now.

There were a number of ways to kill a man. He could be gunned down in the darkness of the street with a slug in the back – the coward's way. Or he could be blasted from long range with a rifle out in the open – another skunk's way to deal out death. The best way with a man like Mick Fulton was to make him go for a gun in front of witnesses.

Garry went up the wide mahogany-railed staircase, taking two steps at a time. No one took any notice of him except the stranger in the blue-serge suit who stood at the bar counter and smilingly watched Garry as he reached the landing on the first floor. Men walked past him in bunches of twos; men who were well-dressed, with gold watch-chains straddling ornate vests. A door opened in the passage and Garry edged to the opening as a man came out. He kept the door half-open with one long arm. He stared keenly around a room which wasn't large but held four tables at which card games were in operation. Drinks and money littered the polished tops of the tables. Garry Maine's gaze swept over them, finally coming to rest on Mick Fulton who was standing with his back to a glowing fire in a large stone fireplace. A girl at his side held a tray of drinks.

Perhaps it was his sixth sense that made the thickset man jerk his head around. As his eyes met Garry Maine's, he dropped his glass. It hit the edge of the stone fireplace and shattered.

Mick Fulton thought he was looking at a man returned from the dead. His mouth worked soundlessly and then he gulped.

Garry Maine walked over the thick carpet. He stood with his feet apart, his hand flicking aside the panel of his coat to reveal the Colt 45. Mick Fulton shook his head, still without speech. Men at the card table began to look up, conscious of this tall, grim-faced man standing over them.

'You wearing a gun, Fulton?' Garry, asked.

'No – no, Maine!' Fulton licked at his lips. 'You – you should be dead! How —'

Garry watched the man in disgust. Softness had eaten into Fulton. Three years ago he'd had enough guts to make a play for the gold with the others. Now he trembled.

'Get a gun, Fulton,' Garry said.

The other men sitting at the table below pushed back their chairs.

One man said, 'Now look here, we've got law in this town . . .'

Garry paid the talker no heed. 'Get a gun, Fulton. I'm calling you out.'

'I'm not taking you on,' Fulton said, his voice trembling. 'You – you can't make me heft a gun. I ain't armed.' He gulped. 'You kill me, Maine, and you'll hang.'

Garry loosened the bandanna around his neck. 'See those marks? You and your two pals tried to lynch me. Three years ago you got me sent to a rotten jail, then you picked up the loot.' He gave a curt laugh. 'You could've gone to prison for taking the gold, Fulton, but I kept quiet and let you get away with it. I was saving you.'

Garry Maine felt every muscle in his body tighten as he recalled the hate that had built up inside him for three long years. There had been tortuous months staring through window bars at the sky . . . the slave conditions of the work party, where the pick and shovel had been weapons he'd been tempted to use on the warders . . . nights of not sleeping while the rotten, gut-filling canker of hatred ate at him, consuming him. There had been nothing in his brain for three years but hate.

'Jail would be too good for you three,' Garry snapped.

'You just want to kill,' Fulton said.

'You got it, Fulton. I want you dead. You and Behan and Kray.'

Eyes bulging, lips dry, Mick Fulton said, 'Look, I was the one who offered you money. Remember? Why – why don't you take the money and let bygones be bygones, huh? I reckon I could get the others to chip in, Maine. Hell, you need money. Killing ain't no good . . . say you'll take the money . . .'

'Damn you!' Garry cried. 'You won't buy off my hate! To hell with you and your money!'

He gazed around the room. All card play had stopped at the four tables. There were no heroes; no man wanted to argue or try to help Mick

Fulton. Garry Maine walked swiftly among the tables until he spotted a man wearing a gun in a holster. He plucked the weapon from the leather and walked back to Fulton. He placed the gun on the table only inches from Fulton's hand. Then Garry backed to his spot near the polished pine wall and waited, face blank.

'Go for the gun,' he said. He flicked back the panel of his coat and suspended his hand a long way from the Colt butt. Fulton had every chance.

But the man didn't make a move. His eyes twitched. His cheeks quivered. Then he said, 'No, no,' pitifully.

A chair rasped on the floor. Garry flung a glance in that direction. It was just a man reacting nervously. A saloon girl gasped, hand to her mouth. Then it was so silent in the room that the hiss of an oil lamp could be heard.

'You're a damned coward,' Garry said.

'I don't reckon to die,' Fulton croaked out.

'I could blast you now, you bastard!'

'It would be murder. You'd hang.'

At that moment the door was pushed open and a young man walked in, a smile on his smooth face, his blue-serge coat open to show his Colt Peacemaker.

'This the place where big money changes hands?' the newcomer asked.

But his gaze was on the gun lying near Fulton's hand, and he'd addressed his words to Garry.

Garry took a deep breath and jerked back the panel of his coat. 'All right, Fulton, you live another day.'

Garry Maine walked past the young man with the Peacemaker, not giving him a second glance. He went out into the passage. When he reached the top of the stairs the smiling young fellow was right behind him.

'I thought you wanted to play cards?' Garry rapped.

'The company seemed a bit ruffled. They were all reaching for drinks. I think something scared them.'

'I did.'

The stranger smiled. 'You looked ready to use your gun on that fat rannigan.'

'Maybe . . .'

'He's Mick Fulton, the owner of the place.'

'I know.'

'Murder is a serious business even in a frontier town like Cedar Springs. I hear they've got a good sheriff by the name of Hec Shield.'

'I don't know him. But then I don't really know this town too well.'

'Just well enough to want to drill Fulton?'

27

Garry Maine paused halfway down the stairs. 'Who the hell are you and why the questions?'

'Me?' The man shrugged. 'I'm here in town on business. The name is Ben Gault. What do I call you?'

'You don't.'

'Care for a drink?'

'Yeah. Alone.'

The other man smiled broadly as they continued down the stairs. 'You know, pal, I think you should think twice about killing that man Fulton. Murder is a nasty business.'

Garry Maine didn't feel like further drinking, despite his words to the man known as Ben Gault. He walked into the night, fuming.

When he was back to his hotel room, he stared long and hard in the mirror above the dresser. He saw his long, angular face, the tight lips, the thick black hair. He knew he looked older than his twenty-six years, and a lot older than Ben Gault, yet their age gap was probably only a couple of years. Why had the man butted in? In town on business? What sort of business?

Garry took off the bandanna and cursed the deep bruises and burn marks on his throat. He figured he'd had enough for one day. He needed sleep. Tomorrow was another day ... and maybe there would be a dead man to mark its passing.

3

A Gunny, a Letter and a Girl

'He's a dangerous young bastard!' raged Luke Behan.

Mick Fulton played with his hat nervously. 'He's after us, no mistake. He'd have killed me last night if I'd gone for that gun . . .'

'But he stopped short of murder,' said Caleb Kray smoothly. 'Of course, it would have been stupid in front of so many witnesses. Well, we're warned . . .' He lowered his gaze thoughtfully to his desk. They were in his office. A rider had gone out earlier to the T Bar T with a message for Luke Behan. 'I wonder how he got free from that noose. We should have stayed there until there was no breath left in his body.'

'That's what I wanted to do,' snapped the rancher.

Kray sighed. 'Well, we've got to finish him. We'll hire a gunny to deal with him – now – today.'

'That's what I had in mind, too,' said Luke Behan. 'God damn it, we can afford to buy the best.'

'We'll see who we can contact,' Kray said. 'You and me, Luke. But we've got to act careful. We don't want to be seen talking to a known gunhand.'

'How about Mick coming along?' Luke Behan argued. 'Do we do all the work?'

Caleb Kray eyed the perspiring saloon owner coldly. 'He's lost his nerve, can't you see that? He'll say the wrong things, maybe give us away. We don't want some jasper figuring he can black-mail us after the job is done. We give no reasons. We just want a man killed – today.'

'All right,' said the rancher grumpily. 'You're right, Mick is no good to us. He figures Maine would take money – a fool notion.'

'He – he – might . . .' said Mick Fulton, resentful of the other's disparaging tone.

'You're getting to be a useless slob, Mick,' sneered Luke Behan. 'Too much damn drink . . . and them skirts hangin' around your place. God, but three years of drinkin' and beddin' has sure made a mess of you.'

'Don't talk to me like that!' It was a shout.

'Keep your voice down,' warned Caleb Kray. 'I've got a clerk in the outer office.'

'You should've got married, like me,' Behan said. 'We settled down in this place . . . all the money we want, sittin' pretty.'

'But you didn't know Maine would be out in three years,' said Mick Fulton. 'And you didn't realize he'd be smart enough to collect information about us while he was in jail. He knew where we went to. Hell, you kept tellin' us that he'd never leave the Pen – that he'd try to escape and get shot – or hit at a warder and pick up another seven years. Yeah, Behan, you told us we were safe forever. But now look – three years and he's found us.'

'You're as nervy as one of your saloon bitches, Fulton,' Behan snapped. 'Get a grip on yourself. Maine will die. Damn it, you were man enough to help grab that gold three years back. Now you've gone soft.'

Caleb Kray got to his feet. 'Quit this damn squabbling! Luke, you come and help me find a gunny. Mick, get back to the Gold Cougar and lock yourself in.'

It was a contemptuous dismissal. Mick Fulton went back to his saloon fuming. There was still enough man in him to feel rage at his cowardice.

33

Behan and Kray were in a rowdy saloon some thirty minutes later, looking for a man whose name had been given to them after a conversation in another saloon.

They found him. Bart Logan, a lean man of medium height dressed in black, right to his stetson, the brim shading cold grey eyes. His gun hung low in a cutaway holster.

Behan looked into the pale face. 'We think you could do a job for us, Logan. Would you care to take a drink with us?'

Behan and Kray went with the man to a table in the rear. The saloon wasn't the kind of place men of means frequented, and the two men had taken a good look around before entering, just to see if there was anyone they knew inside the den.

'A job?' said Bart Logan softly as he reached for the whisky Kray had poured for him.

Luke Behan nodded. 'We won't beat around the bush. There's a man in town we'd like dead – today, before he gives us any trouble. Do you understand?'

The gunman shrugged. 'Death comes to all of us, gentlemen. But for a premature end, someone has to pay. Is this man well-known in town?'

'He's a nobody. We'll point him out to you.'

'All in good time,' said Logan. 'A nobody? Then

34

not too many questions will be asked by the law. Why do you want this man dead?'

'Well, that's our business,' said Caleb Kray. 'He's a nuisance, and we think death is the only way to handle him.'

The gunman's pale face was thoughtful. 'I guess it's just a business deal, then, gentlemen. But even nobodys come expensive.'

'All right,' said Caleb Kray. 'How much?'

'A thousand dollars.'

'That's damn high!'

'The service is for both of you, I take it. Well, I say it's cheap at five hundred dollars. Don't you agree?'

Kray and Behan looked at each other and then nodded. 'We'll have to show you the, er, victim,' muttered Caleb Kray. 'We can't be seen going down Main Street together, as I'm sure you can understand. How long have you been in town, Logan?'

'Too long. I'm movin' on – soon.'

'Suits us,' said Luke Behan. 'We'll pay you when the man concerned is dead.'

'I want half now,' said the gunman. 'When I get the other half, I ride out.'

Caleb Kray, his legal mind ticking over, thought this man was a good choice. If he rode out, there would be no unpleasant complications, like Logan asking for more money and making embarrassing calls at the office.

Nudging Luke Behan's arm, Kray stood up. 'Let's go. We'll show you this drifter we want dead. We've found out he's staying at a cheap hotel. We'll show you . . .'

The two men were acutely aware of their importance in the town. Behan, a member of the Cattleman's Association, enjoyed the regular meetings which were largely drinking sessions with people in the same trade. Kray was a member of a club which held regular get togethers at which both politics and business were discussed – again with the aid of drinks – and only the influential men of Cedar Springs were members. So they were wary of being seen walking the streets of the busy town with a man whose craft was stamped on his face, his attire and his cutaway holster. So Kray elected to show the gunhand the hotel where Garry Maine was staying. Luke Behan disappeared in the direction of the Gold Cougar, needing a drink.

Caleb Kray stood close to a shop front, trying to appear interested in the merchandise displayed in the small window. He had his back to the street. Bart Logan stood near him, close enough to hear his comments.

'That's the hotel, friend. This drifter is a big

man who wears a sheepskin coat, a battered hat and rides a big black stallion. He packs a gun and he's pretty good with it. He's got black hair and a kind of lean, sharp face. Where he is right now I don't know – but maybe you'll see him leave or enter this hotel.'

'You tell me plenty except his name.'

'Garry Maine.'

'What's he doin' in town?'

'I've told you – he drifted here.'

Bart Logan's cold eyes flickered. 'All right, you don't pay good cash just to fix a nobody, but I guess your reasons are your own business.' He paused, then he stabbed hard at Kray's ribs with his finger. 'Just get it straight, mister. I collect the second payment in that saloon as soon as you hear the news – or you and your pard will pick up real grief.'

Kray nodded and said, 'Follow me – and stay about fifteen yards behind. I'm going to get you the money. Stand on the boardwalk opposite the Mercantile Bank. I'll come out with the money and hand it over when I figure nobody is taking any notice. You got all that?'

'Sure.'

Within around fifteen minutes the deal was concluded. Caleb Kray went to join Luke Behan in the Gold Cougar. Bart Logan sauntered along

Main Street, a wad of bills inside his shirt. He knew he would have to quickly carry out the bargain if he wanted the second instalment. There wasn't one reason why he shouldn't dispose of a lone drifter. It was just a question of identifying him and then waiting for the right moment.

Caleb Kray called in at his office before he rejoined Luke Behan in the Gold Cougar. His clerk handed him a letter, a long envelope which had no stamp or postmark on it.

'Handed in, sir, by a boy. It's addressed to you and marked personal . . .'

'I can see that.' Kray treated his underlings like dirt. As a very young man he'd had to suffer insults from superiors while studying law, and he had never forgotten it. He had failed his law course and had headed West, where such details were not so important, and he'd practised as a lawyer in many towns, never with great success. There had been years of this and then he'd met Behan and Fulton – and Garry Maine. Then there was the gold.

'The letter is probably from someone in town, Mr Kray,' volunteered the clerk. 'It hasn't gone through the post office.'

'I don't pay you to make obvious observations,' said Caleb Kray thinly. 'Get back to your work.'

As the man went away with bowed shoulders, Kray slit open the letter. He stared at the written lines, noting there was no signature. Then he read:

Dear Mr Kray: This is simply to let you know I am interested in you, your two friends Behan and Fulton, and your enmity towards a man called Garry Maine, who was recently released from the State Penitentiary at Butte, Montana. But more than that, I'm highly intrigued by the mention of the word 'gold'. I think you, too, are interested in gold – as are your two friends. I have been making some inquiries about you three. It seems you were not so well-to-do in Powder River City where you lived just before moving to Cedar Springs. In fact, you became wealthy – along with your friends – just after Maine went to prison. I know he was accused of robbing a wagon carrying gold from the Powder River mine, but he did not do it single-handed. You will be seeing me soon. Incidentally, please destroy this letter. I am sure you will.

Caleb Kray, pale with anger under his tan, hurried to the Gold Cougar where he showed the letter to Behan and Fulton. They went to a private room upstairs.

'What the hell is this?' Luke Behan exclaimed. 'It – it's impossible! I mean, who the hell could know all this?'

'It was handed in by a boy at my office,' stated Kray. 'So the writer is in town. My guess is that he knows a little but not too much.'

'God, another worry,' moaned Mick Fulton.

Caleb Kray tapped the sheet of paper. 'I'll make some inquiries. Maybe my clerk can find the boy who handed this in and he'll describe the man. Anyway, this fellow is sure to reveal himself eventually because it's obvious he wants a payoff.'

Luke Behan's eyes gleamed. 'Right. We'll handle him. He ain't the law, that's for sure. The minute we get to know who he is, we can deal with him.'

'We'll get the gunny to blast him,' said Mick Fulton eagerly, as if the matter was as good as taken care of. 'I don't mind payin'.'

'You're going to pay towards the price of gettin' rid of Maine,' snarled Behan. 'And you can do some goddamn work. It's risky contacting galoots like this Bart Logan. Folks talk . . . we can't be seen with a gunhand . . .'

Caleb Kray walked around the room, the leanest of the three in a fine city suit, his hawk-like face tight. 'Logan might be useful – but we've got to watch out that we don't collect a blackmailer. I guess he'll take care of Maine, so we don't have to worry about that any more.'

Luke Behan was puzzled. 'Now who wrote that letter – that's what baffles me. Have you noticed any curious characters around town lately?'

Kray threw him a cynical smile. 'This place is full of curious characters. Every day the stages bring more – gamblers – Easterners – carpet-baggers – family men – saloon girls. All strangers. I figure the writer of this letter is a stranger to Cedar Springs . . . and well-educated. Notice the neat writing. It's certainly not the work of some saddletramp.'

Luke Behan nodded and walked the length of the room, his hands behind his back. 'Fine, Kray. Keep up your reasonin' and we might get a clue.'

'This man might have a few notions about us – but that ain't proof,' said Mick Fulton. 'We've just got to tell him to go to hell. What can he do?'

Luke Behan stopped his pacing to glare. 'We don't ever want his crazy notions put in front of the law. Suspicions stick to you like dirt. And Hec Shield is smart. We're businessmen, accepted in this town – and it's gonna stay that way.'

Caleb Kray summed it up: 'We can't do much

until this fellow gives us a clue to his identity. Then maybe it'll cost us another thousand.'

The other two nodded in agreement. It would pay them to keep Bart Logan on hand.

Garry Maine awakened late in the morning and ate a hearty breakfast. It was a distinct improvement over prison grub and a lot better than the scratch meals he'd had on the trail. Then, fully fed and thoughtful, he decided to strike. He would hit at a man who wouldn't be too frightened to go for his gun. That man was Luke Behan. Caleb Kray was craftier, and would have to be cornered before he would fight, but Behan had always worn a hogleg. For the moment Mick Fulton was reprieved.

Garry rode out to the T Bar T spread. He looked a typical range rider with his bedroll and saddlebags, rifle scabbard and water canteen.

He didn't know he was being followed. Bart Logan was adept at trailing a man.

The T Bar T was fairly close to town, the first of a half-dozen spreads that radiated from Cedar Springs like gigantic spokes that thrust into the wooded valleys and hills of the area. On the highest pine-clad hills were lumber camps. Swinging axes bit deep into the timber and the logs came bumping down the river to a catchment area just before the rapids at Cedar Springs. There was a big sawmill on the outskirts of town. Huge wagons hauled cut timber to the railroad and to towns as far as thirty miles away, where the flatlands were almost entirely grass.

Garry Maine pictured Luke Behan somewhere on his ranch. He didn't know where he would find the man; he'd just keep looking. He'd stick around until Behan showed up. If necessary he would sit on a pole fence until the man appeared, then he would rile him into going for his gun. Now, rolling with the stallion's gait, he felt the thrill of freedom and he had to remind himself that revenge was his most important consideration. Then he told himself that he'd feel the old hatred again the moment he sighted Luke Behan. Yes, that was all he needed.

He didn't realize that the man he wanted dead was back at Cedar Springs. He hadn't known that the three men had met that morning in Kray's office.

Behind Garry, Bart Logan knew it would be easy to ambush his man and leave him dead with a Winchester slug in his back. But the lean man in the black garb had a curious sort of pride. He figured he was one of the fastest gunhandlers in the Montana Territory and so could easily handle the tall drifter.

43

Garry Maine was within shouting distance of the T Bar T when he heard hoofbeats behind him. He turned to look and saw the girl astride a chestnut, whip in hand.

'You again,' he said. 'You sure look at home with that whip.'

Her blue eyes gleamed at him, ready to accept a challenge. She was wearing the blue jeans and a cord jacket. Her long blonde hair flowed down to her back. Eyes gleaming, a smile on her red lips, she cracked the whip.

'You were told not to come back here,' she said. 'Maybe I should use the whip on you this time.'

He leaned on the saddle pommel. 'I wouldn't advise it. Maybe I'd have to give you a damn good walloping – somethin' you seem to be begging for, lady.'

'You're on T Bar T land. I could shout for men who'd run you off.'

'That's different.' He chased the amusement out of his face. 'Your father anywhere around?'

'He is not.'

'Go get him, Miss.'

Her anger began to rise. 'Who the devil are you?'

'I'm called Garry Maine. Who are you, Miss – apart from bein' Behan's daughter?'

'I'm his stepdaughter, as I told you last time.

Now move on, drifter, before I do whip you. I haven't forgotten your insolence.'

'You were giving your bad temper a workout,' he said. 'You were hitting a defenceless Indian. You have got a name?'

She jigged her horse around. For a moment her whip arm was raised and Garry thought she was going to strike at him, but with an effort she controlled herself, her cheeks tinged with pink.

'You are the most insufferable man I've ever met!' she flared.

He grinned. 'You've sure got some fury in you. Do you ever get calm? What's with you, Miss? Or do I just rile you by lookin' at you?'

'You – you're utterly insolent! That's what's wrong with you. And you've got no right to be here.'

'I want to see Luke Behan.' Just saying the name made him go grim again. He cursed his mission momentarily.

'Why? Do you need a job?' She had calmed swiftly, seeing that she could taunt him. 'I'm sure you're big enough to do some honest work, such as cleaning out the stables or fixing fences – something simple and requiring no mental effort.'

'I just want to see him. Get him out here.' Harshness thickened his voice. He knew he was glaring at the girl, and there was no real reason apart from her silly display of temper and arrogance.

'Well, I'm Lucia Ward – although my mother is now Mrs Behan. I guess I can humour you. Luke Behan isn't here. He's gone to Cedar Springs.'

At this moment Bart Logan rode his horse carefully between two high knolls and then reined up to look at Garry Maine and the girl. He was positioned just right for a fast draw.

'Is this man annoying you, Miss?' Logan asked.

4

Man in a Cooler

Bart Logan sat his horse coolly, his eyes not leaving Garry Maine's face. He was searching for the change of expression that came over most men when they were about to go for a handgun. But then he realized that a lot more prodding was needed to push this man to a draw. At the moment Maine saw him merely as a nuisance. The man would have to be riled. And it was a known fact that anger affected speed and judgment.

'You're pushin' yourself on this gal, ain't you?' Logan said. 'I saw you. Big man, accosting a girl . . .'

Garry held his reins lightly in one hand, giving the man a long, keen study. There was the fancy holster. He noted, too, the pale, uncalloused hands. This man did no manual work.

47

'We were just talking,' Garry said quietly.

'You damn liar! A big guy. Fancy yourself a real dude with women, eh?' Logan sneered. 'You were arguing – pushing yourself on to this girl. Where I come from that ain't gentlemanly.'

'Where do you come from?' asked Garry smoothly.

'What's that to you?' The belligerence in Logan's tone was unmistakable, but he was inwardly cool. 'I don't like your ways, mister.'

Garry Maine smiled at Lucia Ward and then at Logan. Looking again at the girl, he said, 'Tell this gent I wasn't annoying you. Then he might crawl back under his rock.'

'I don't have to do you any favours, Mr Maine.'

'You could tell this rannigan to ride on. Tell him you don't need his help. Maybe he'll apologise and take that crowbait horse of his out of here.'

The girl glanced at the gunhand. 'Please, there's no need for trouble. Thank you for your offer of assistance, but I don't need anyone to help me.' She flashed a glance at Garry. 'I can handle this man.'

Bart Logan stared, poker-faced. In spite of his professional desire to stay cool he felt a tinge of anger at the way Maine had spoken so contemptuously. But he had to kill this tall man coldly, efficiently. False anger was one thing, but real annoyance was dangerous.

'This galoot has a loose mouth,' Logan snapped. 'I don't like it.'

Garry flicked him a glance. Warnings flashed through his brain. This man in black was undoubtedly a gunhand; no need for doubt on that point. He sent another glance at the man's holster and then met his cold eyes again.

'Are you trying to pick a fight?' Garry asked.

'I just don't like the way you talk back.'

'Too bad. I'll say it again – ride off and mind your own business. I was having a talk with Miss Ward and you don't figure in it.'

'I still say you've got a loose mouth, big man.'

'Why don't you leg down from that horse and put up your fists if you're so determined to argue?'

'We've got guns.'

And at that moment Garry Maine knew the man in black was a hired gun. His attempt to prod him was too obvious. He'd been hired by Kray, Behan and Fulton. That was it; they figured to get rid of him with a hired gun.

Garry felt the old hatred run right through every nerve in his body. Three men had sent him to jail and had tried to hang him; now they'd sent this gunslinger after him. The man wasn't here by mere chance; he'd followed him from Cedar Springs.

The girl jigged her restless horse around as the men held tight leathers on their animals. Lucia Ward cried out: 'Just what is this all about? Who is this man?'

'A gunhand,' said Garry. He could have added that her stepfather had sent the man after him.

'So you've got enemies, big man?'

'You can say that again.' But Garry didn't take his narrow-eyed gaze from the face of the man in black.

'No doubt you're a trouble-maker,' she said. 'Well, I'm going back to the ranch.'

But she didn't have time to turn her horse. Bart Logan, confident of his fast draw, said, 'Reach for iron, mister.'

With only seconds in which to save his life, Garry Maine knew he'd have to pull an old trick. He had been in prison three years – and the authorities did not allow jailbirds to play with guns. He'd strapped on his gun outside the penitentiary gates; they were that strict. It was a useful gun and holster. Only a few men wore his kind of gun gear.

On the three days' ride to Cedar Springs he'd spent a bit of time getting used to the feel of the holster again. He'd spent ten minutes every few hours practising the swing of the leather. He'd also made a few conventional fast draws – but he knew he was slow.

Garry Maine knew there was only one hope for him. He didn't draw his gun. He jerked his big body as if a steel spring activated his spine, then his right hand swivelled the leather holster. As Logan's gun appeared in his hand as if by magic, Garry's finger sought the trigger in the notch cut into the holster. The levelled gun fired – just before Logan's gun barked a useless slug into the sky.

The trick holster swivelled on a greased rivet attached to Garry's gunbelt. The holster was merely a covering for the gun.

The bullet hit Bart Logan in the upper thigh. That was one of the drawbacks with the swivel holster; the slug usually went low. But it was always faster than the draw the most competent of gunmen could achieve.

With another swift motion Garry whipped his gun free of leather. Logan was leaning back, his left leg buckling. Garry legged down from his horse and let the frightened animal jig away. As Logan rolled in his saddle in pain, Garry grabbed the gun from his hand. A second later he unseated the man, heaving his good leg out of the stirrup and giving him a push that sent him thudding to the earth.

The horses milled around in fright. The girl kept her mount under control and, startled, watched Garry Maine stand over the fallen gunhand.

'You're not dead, mister, and you'll walk again,' snapped Garry. 'Now you don't have to tell me who sent you – I know. Just get the hell out of here.'

'I'll kill you, Maine.' The threat hissed from a mouth twisted with pain. 'You're making a mistake letting me live.'

'Maybe you're right.' Garry raised his Colt a fraction.

'It would be murder,' snarled the man.

'Would it? But you figured to prod me into going for my gun, knowing you could beat any ordinary draw. If you'd killed me, would that be murder?'

'The girl here would be witness to a fair fight.'

'Is that so? Well, head back, gunslinger, and tell them you failed.' Garry shoved the man's gun under his own belt. Let the gunny pay out for another weapon; maybe that and the wound in the thigh might change his mind about another try. Garry walked a few yards to get Logan's horse. He took Logan's rifle from the saddle scabbard and led the animal back to the hobbling gunfighter.

'Get! Tell them you were unlucky.'

'I'll kill you!' It wasn't an idle threat. Bart Logan was stating what to him was a fact. 'I'll kill you.'

Garry nodded, then he watched the man mount with some effort and ride away. Then he turned to the girl.

'Who is he?' she asked.

'I don't know his name, but he knows mine.'

'Why did he try to kill you?'

'Paid.'

'Don't exert yourself trying to explain,' she said. 'And you need not come to the ranch – there's no work for troublemakers here. Anyway, Luke Behan is in town, as I told you.'

'I can believe that now.'

'What do you mean by that?'

Garry grinned coldly. 'Forget it, Miss Ward. Your stepfather isn't around, but I haven't had a ride out for nothing – I've met you again. And that's mighty interesting because you're some girl.'

'You're trying to infuriate me again.' But her desire to rise to the bait was cut short because at that moment two riders in range attire came up to them at a fast lope.

As they stopped their animals on sliding rear hoofs, one man called out, 'We heard shots.

What's goin' on, Miss Ward? Was it this man?'

She hesitated. Then, triumphantly, 'He's a drifter asking for my stepfather. Run him off, boys.'

She didn't understand why she felt rage towards this tall man in the trail-stained garb. It was there all the time and had been that way from the first moment she'd met him. She felt compelled to be defiant with him, even outrageously badtempered. Yet she was conscious of a remote desire to prove to him that she wasn't always impossible and ill-mannered.

The two cowhands were hard men. They surveyed Garry Maine with distrust, noting the regular gun in his holster, the second weapon under his belt, and the two rifles in his saddle scabbard.

Garry smiled back, feeling no enmity towards them. But it was a state of mind destined to be short-lived.

One of the men said, 'We've got a cooler for trespassers, Miss – remember?'

'Yeah, that's the boss's orders – the cooler for intruders,' the second hand put in.

She nodded. Then a lariat went out and rope circled Garry Maine's shoulders, biting into his arms just around the elbows.

The rope tightened. Garry had no desire to

shoot at cowhands just doing a job, so he contented himself with bracing against the rope. He said, 'Get this damn rope off me. I'll go.'

'Yeah, to the cooler.'

The girl laughed as another loop snaked out and fell around Garry. He turned to Lucia Ward.

'Tell them to get their ropes off me! I'll ride back to town – that's a promise.'

'I think the cooler is just made for you,' she said, laughing. 'It will teach you respect for others, drifter.'

'Why, you spoiled brat!' he cried, his rage spilling out. 'Some day I'll beat that damned rump of yours!'

The ropes pulled at him as the hands urged their horses forward. He was towed along like a trussed steer, his stallion obeying the tug. He sat the saddle, his thighs pressed hard against the animal's ribs, rolling as the horses went into a gallop. The riders went fast into the ranch yard and circled a barn where two grinning men stopped their work to watch, then they drew up at a small log hut.

'The cooler,' said one man.

They didn't give him a chance to reach a gun. One hand poked an old Colt at Garry as the other undid the lariats. Then the door of the log hut was opened. The girl looked on, still laughing

55

when Garry was pushed into the hut. The door was fastened with a bar on the outside.

Garry was in a cell. Without windows, it was only big enough for a man to stand up or squat on his haunches. Cooler? It was boiling hot.

Lucia Ward said, 'You can stay in there for a few hours, Mr Maine. I'm sure it will teach you a lesson. Maybe you'll show more respect – something a drifter should have. Anyway, the laugh is on you. We'll hitch your horse outside so when you're released you'll be able to ride out, hopefully in a more humble frame of mind.'

'You brat!' he yelled back. 'You need tanning within an inch of your life! Let me out now – pronto!'

'Use your strength to fight your way out,' was her taunting reply. 'I'm going.'

Garry was trapped. No man could break down the heavy door or smash his way through six-inch pine logs. They had left him with his guns, but he could use them only when they released him, and no doubt they would then make sure he was covered.

It was stupid of him to get into this mess by tangling with the girl. Of course, she had no idea her stepfather was out to kill Garry. Nor did she know that he'd vowed to put an end to Luke Behan's life.

After futile kicks at the pine logs, Garry began to examine the cell. The joints between the logs were filled with clay. The floor was hard earth. Staring down, he wondered how far the logs went into the ground. Could a man dig under the frame of the cell?

He squatted down and began to scoop up the soil. He dug down one side of the wall for about a foot, sweating heavily. He had to stop work for a while to get his breath. Then he began again, and finally he felt at the bottom of the frame, a little more than eighteen inches down.

The difficulty now lay in disposing of the soil. He piled it up on the far side of the cell but it began to run down again. Within an hour he had a hole in which he could stand. He was covered in dirt and his hands were raw and bleeding. For once he wished he wasn't so big.

He had to rest. He sat in the hole, his two guns in a corner where soil wouldn't get in the barrels or mechanisms. He went back to work. With his exertions the heat in the confined space became almost insufferable, and the running soil began to trickle back into the hole as fast as he built it up behind him. Progress was now agonisingly difficult. He had to rest frequently, cursing the pile of red soil behind him that sloped up to the wall of the cell. Then he scooped again, red soil and sand, gravel and stone coming his way. His head was down in the hole. He was bent double.

Twice he almost decided to wait until they freed him. He had guns, but of course they would be ready with their weapons. It wasn't worth killing or maiming just because of this trick played on him. He didn't want to kill ranch hands.

Then he snarled his rage at his predicament. He blamed the girl. She could have ordered the hands to let him go.

He scooped savagely for a few more minutes. Then he was clawing upward, outside the logs. He lay on his back and scooped, spitting out soil as it fell around his head. He burrowed, eyes and nose full of dirt, his hat and guns still inside the log cell. He couldn't go back; he was throwing earth behind him, partially blocking his return. He had to dig on and on.

Suddenly the ground above fell around him and he could see daylight. He cursed and pushed out of the hole, rolling on to the flat ground close to the log cell door. At the side of the small hut his horse was tethered. The animal jigged as Garry staggered to his feet and leaned against the pine logs. He wasted no time, glancing around to see if he'd been observed. The nearest men were a long way off, at a horse corral. He turned to the cell door, lifted the bar, entered and collected his hat and the guns.

He hit the saddle and rode out fast, sending the stallion leaping over the yard rail. It was only then that men on the ranch noticed his escape. He headed at an all-out gallop towards a screening stand of timber. As the horse entered the trees, he slowed him down to a walk. Ten minutes later he discovered a spring bubbling into a rocky pool.

Hitching the horse, he took off his gunbelt and clothes and stood there, naked, warm air playing on his back. He picked up his Colt and carefully placed it on a rock ledge over the pool. Then he waded into the water, grinning as the coolness hit him. He splashed around for some minutes, ready to reach out for the gun at the slightest sound. When all the dirt was gone he waded from the pool.

He knew what he had to do now. He'd wait until Luke Behan returned to the ranch, then somehow he'd get him. He filled in time with a number of chores – cleaning his clothes, seeing that his gun was free of dirt, allowing his horse to water. He was not too hungry after the large breakfast he'd had in town, so he contented himself with hard biscuits from his saddle-bag and water from the spring. Then he led the horse to the fringe of the timber and watched the distant ranch.

He noted the arrival of a wagon which probably carried supplies, then he saw two separate groups of riders go slowly down the trail to the ranch, the men and horses looking tired. But he didn't see Luke Behan. Then a woman walked from the house and stood at the main gate. Even at this distance Garry knew she wasn't the tall blonde girl. She seemed older. Was this the girl's mother?

Filled with anger, he thought about the way Luke Behan had built up a secure life for himself on gold that Garry had helped him steal. There he was, the owner of a prosperous ranch, with probably some of the gold still salted away, for the yellow metal was better than money in the bank. A man on the run could take gold if he wasn't able to visit his bank. Behan had all this, and even a wife and daughter. Kray had respect as a lawyer, and Fulton his money-spawning saloon. Maybe all of them still had gold salted away.

Watching the woman, he got the impression she was waiting. And she was. Soon a man in a town suit and a black hat rode down the trail, coming from the east, the direction of Cedar Springs. The man was Luke Behan.

Garry Maine waited. The sun was setting. Maybe the right time to approach the ranch house was after dark. He'd waited for three years to kill Behan; he could spare a few more hours.

5

The Fatal Slug

Luke Behan was sitting with Lucia and his wife, Kate, in the huge living room of the T Bar T ranch house, his face set thoughtfully as he stared at the crackling log fire. There was fresh trouble to ponder over as Lucia told of the fight between Garry Maine and the gunhand, and the way the cowboys had rounded up the tall man and placed him in the cooler.

'He was looking for you, Dad. A man named Garry Maine. He pulled a neat trick on this man in black . . .'

'I guess he did,' gritted Luke Behan.

'Do you know this man?'

Some kind of explanation had to be offered. Kate Behan's shrewd grey eyes were on her husband. She was just over forty, and had been widowed when Lucia was a child in pigtails. She was grateful now for security.

'Maine is a damned trouble-maker,' said Luke Behan. 'Keep away from him, Lucia.' He paused; he could have added that Garry Maine mightn't live long enough for her to get to know him. 'He's dangerous.'

'He escaped from the cooler,' she said. 'I think that was amazing. I let the men put him there for – well, a joke.'

'Did he say anything to you about why he'd called at the ranch?' Luke Behan waited guardedly for her reply.

'Well, no . . . Just that he wanted to see you. Then this man in black came. It was frightening the way they went for their guns.'

'He's a young hellion who collects enemies,' Behan said. 'Maybe the man in black had good reason for calling him out.'

Lucia fell silent as she caught her mother's glance. There were questions in her mind, but perhaps it was wiser not to ask. Lucia didn't mention that she'd met Garry Maine earlier, when he had taken the whip from her. Actually, she was ashamed of that episode.

At that moment Sam Roper entered the room. He was the T Bar T ramrod, a hardcase who knew nothing of Luke Behan's earlier history. He halted, legs apart, a hand on his gunbutt. He had time before he spoke to flick a greedy glance at Lucia Ward and admire the shapely body under her flowing dress.

'There's a damned snooper outside, boss. He's on a big black hoss just beyond the fence. He stops to stare at the ranch house every few minutes.'

'A tall galoot?'

'Seems a big feller, yeah. I yelled out to him and he rode into the darkness, then he came back a bit later.'

Luke Behan got to his feet. To his credit, he had guts, and anger always thrust him into action. 'Get some hands – men who can use a gun. I'll come with you. We'll run this spy off the ranch – or shoot him dead.'

'Dead, boss?'

Behan's glinting eyes challenged the foreman. 'He's a trespasser – maybe a horse-thief. You don't argue with horse thieves.'

In the Montana Territory a horse-thief was always a good reason for shooting. He was prepared to explain even to Sheriff Hec Shield that he'd figured he was dealing with a horse thief if Garry Maine ended up dead. He had no doubt it was Maine.

Sam Roper slapped the butt of his handgun.

'I'll get the men.'

'Fine. And get my horse. Have it ready outside the patio.'

Luke Behan walked to a chest of drawers, opened the biggest and took out a gunbelt. A Colt lay in the holster. When he had the belt around his waist, he took out the gun and checked the cylinder.

'You're going out to hunt this man?' Kate Behan asked in a tone that suggested disapproval.

'We'll teach him,' said Behan savagely.

'But maybe he'll just ride off. It's dangerous for you to act like a gunman. Why not send for the sheriff?'

He smiled. 'You worried, Kate? You'd be a rich widow if I got killed.'

'You're a fool to talk like that,' she said. 'And a bigger fool to attempt to use a gun. You're not cut out for it.'

He moved to the door, holding back a smile. True, he'd never been a real gunhand, but some of the deals he'd pulled with Kray and Fulton had needed guns as persuasion. And then had come the big one, the chance in a lifetime that had set them up for life, with Maine the scapegoat to take the blame.

He met Sam Roper outside the ranch house

and mounted the horse the ramrod held for him. There were four other men, young hands not averse to a bit of tough action.

As they rode through the main gate, a clear voice hailed them from the darkness:

'Hey – Behan – over here. Let's see how much guts you've got left.'

It was Garry Maine's voice. But there was nothing to see in the inky blackness beyond the yellow light thrown by the last lantern hanging in the ranch yard. The six men rode out in a bunch.

'Who is this loco galoot?' asked one man. 'There are six of us to his one gun.'

'Shoot him dead!' snapped the ramrod. 'He's a damn hoss thief. You've got nothin' to fear from the law.'

Thus encouraged, the hardcases began to fan out once clear of the ranch yard fence, but Luke Behan wasn't about to take stupid chances.

'Stay with me,' he said to Sam Roper. 'The two of us will get this rannigan.'

The other man peered into the darkness. 'Black as a Pawnee's scalp. Where's he gone?'

Then Maine's mocking voice rang through the night air again, 'Hey, Behan, you know I want just you. Send these men back to the bunkhouse.'

Sam Roper pointed. 'He's over there. Hell,

boss, he's out to rile you. Who is he?'

'A nobody!' grated Behan. 'Shoot when you see him.'

'He's somewhere between those grassy knolls,' decided Sam Roper, prodding his horse in the direction of the humps of rock and earth, with Luke Behan right behind him. Handguns were held tightly. The two men closed in on the black humps that rose from the gentle slopes like refuse heaps thrown by a giant hand and grassed over by nature. It suddenly occurred to Luke Behan that he was relying on only Sam Roper, for the other hands had taken a wide loop around the knolls.

The two men rode carefully between the big black humps. Then things happened quickly. A big black shape leaped down from a knoll and thudded into Sam Roper.

As Garry Maine landed on the man, Roper's horse reared in fear, forelegs flailing at the air. The two men thudded to the ground, but Sam Roper was beneath Garry and was knocked unconscious. Garry stared up at Luke Behan.

'Three years, Behan. And you tried to hang me . . .' Behan triggered his gun, fear in his bowels. His aim was poor. He hadn't allowed for the movement of his horse. The bullet dug into the earth a yard from Garry Maine. Behan squeezed the trigger again, but Garry had rolled on the slope, head tucked in, gun in hand.

Still Garry Maine didn't fire. Instead he snapped grimly, 'You sent a gunny to deal with me.'

'Damn you, Maine!' cried Luke Behan. 'You've got hell's own luck!' And he sent the rest of the shots in his gun at the dark target.

But Garry had dived behind the unconscious body of Sam Roper. Again the shots missed. Then there was a loud click as the hammer of Behan's gun struck a used shell.

Garry jumped to his feet.

'You had your chance, Behan.' He brought his gun up slowly and triggered once. The Colt barked and the slug tore a hole through Luke Behan's heart. For what seemed a long time to Garry, Behan sat his saddle. Then his nerveless fingers dropped the empty gun.

A second later he slipped lifelessly from the saddle and hit the ground.

Garry stood over the man and touched him with his boot. For a moment he couldn't believe he'd killed Behan. Then a strange feeling came over him. So the man was dead. Did he feel better? He did not.

Then he sensed that the ramrod was stirring. He took the man's gun and threw it away. As it landed it exploded, evidently triggered by a rock. He looked down at Behan again, unwilling to realize that there was no longer a need to hate this man. Then he knew he had to get his horse and ride out. The cowhands had heard the shots. Returning hoofbeats told him they were converging on the grassy knolls.

Garry Maine left the scene on the black stallion just as the first hands got within sighting distance of him in the gloom. Shots were fired, but wildly, hastily. They sang past Garry Maine, then he vanished into the night.

He reached the stand of timber and reined the hard-breathing horse into cover, then he turned and looked back. He saw the lights of the ranch house and heard shouts, although the ranch yard was nearly a mile away.

Luke Behan had paid the penalty for a double-cross that had given one man a prison sentence while Behan and his two friends enjoyed affluence. And he had paid for the attempted hanging and for hiring a gunhand to do his dirty work.

Garry took the trail back to Cedar Springs. As he reached town, where lights still flooded out from the saloons, he knew Caleb Kray and Mick Fulton would soon learn the fate of their partner – and so would the sheriff.

He wasn't worried about what Kray and

Fulton might say to the law in Cedar Springs because they had plenty to hide. Still, they would be interrogated because it was well known in town that the three men were close, and the sheriff would want their opinion about the shooting of Luke Behan. Of course, Lucia Ward would guess at the identity of the 'spy' her stepfather and his hands had gone out to chase. And the two cowboys who'd thrown him in the cooler could identify him.

Without caring a damn, Garry went to bed that night in the hotel, a chair under the doorknob and the key turned in the lock. He had not forgotten the gunhand in black.

Garry Maine went into the sunshine of Main Street the next day, still wearing his red shirt and sheepskin coat. He was aware that he looked like a saddlebum.

He had stashed the gunhand's Colt in his bedroom along with the spare rifle. A man never knew when he might need a spare gun.

He sauntered along the street. Men and women were out and about. Freighters were lined up at the depots, and men pulled at the ribbons of two-horse teams. A stage was loading, the driver on top with some valises and carpetbags on the rack. In a back alley some kids played a noisy game. Just ahead of Garry a black cat tore across the road, chased by an excited dog. And then a two-wheeled gig hauled by a fine, high-stepping horse rolled down the main stem and came to a halt before Garry Maine on the boardwalk.

The girl stepped down from the gig, anger across her fine, clear-skinned face. She strode over to him without a second's hesitation, leaving the ribbons trailing, a horsewhip in a gloved hand. Long strides, fast and lithe, as female as a ballet dancer, brought her up to Garry Maine. As she halted, her long floral calico dress swished around her ankles.

'You – you murderer!'

He stood warily, hating this encounter, cursing the whole situation. She wasted no more epithets, raising her whip so swiftly the action took Garry by surprise.

Then she was whipping him on the head and shoulders. His battered hat flew off, a gust of wind taking it along the hard-baked road. He lurched back, arms up to protect his face. The whip lashed at him while she hissed her hatred.

'You killer! You shot Luke Behan last night! And you'll hang – after I've finished with you!'

There was no alternative to taking the punishment except running or threatening her with a sixgun. He contemplated neither. He grabbed at the whip eventually and wrested it from her hand while his own temper blazed to equal hers. Holding her hands in his rough grip, he shook her hard.

'It was him or me! Can you understand that?'

She shouted, 'You're a dirty murderer.'

'He hired that gunman to kill me. You saw that incident, so you'll be my witness.'

'You're also a liar!'

'Maybe you'll tell me why you're so sore,' he said, glancing around at the onlookers who'd gathered. 'You had no love for Behan.'

'My mother married him – and she was a good wife. She had respect for him.'

'Behan was a rogue!' he snapped. 'He tricked me. I did three years in the Penitentiary because of him and two others.'

'You're lying.'

'Maybe I'll tell you all about it,' he said, 'if I ever get the time. Behan bought that ranch with stolen gold – and that's all I'll tell you right now, Miss Ward.'

She quit struggling and said, 'Sam Roper is with the sheriff right now. The hands will swear you killed Luke Behan. You've got no chance.'

'Is that so? Waal, you, for one, can tell the law that Behan came out gunnin' for me last night with a party of men. I reckon I just hit back in self-defence.'

'You were trespassing. Sam Roper says you're a horse thief. They'll swear you were on T Bar T land to steal – and that's all any jury in Cedar Springs will need to know.'

'You won't make a statement on my behalf?'

'Why should I?'

He released her hands. 'Who's the liar now?' he said.

She glared at him and stepped back. 'You – you're an impossible man. You always make me lose my temper. I – I don't know what it is . . .'

'You just naturally fly off the handle, Miss Lucia.'

She tried to calm herself. 'You're in big trouble. The law will grab you and you'll be tried for murder. And I won't testify in your favour. I'm the only one who can say that Behan and his men went gunning for you last night.'

'That's right.'

'You killed him,' she said. 'Don't you have any remorse?'

'Not much.'

'The law will get you. I figure you've got about ten minutes of freedom left. You must know the sheriff will be after you.'

'I figure there are two men in town who might intervene to say that Luke Behan hired a gunhand to kill me, and that I just fought back

74

in self-defence,' he said calmly.

She was astonished. 'Two men! Who?'

'No names at the moment. These careful gents just don't want to have lawmen askin' awkward questions, and so they might agree to back me up.'

'Two men. Do I know them?'

'Maybe. But that doesn't matter. I was figuring on paying them a visit when you butted in.'

'They must be friends of yours.'

'Not exactly. In fact, it might choke them to back me up. But then when the stink dies down they'll plan on ways to kill me.'

She'd gone quiet, round-eyed. Then, shaking her head in confusion, she returned to her gig.

At that moment a young man in an immaculate fawn suit stepped along the boardwalk. Moving through the onlookers, he walked up to Garry Maine and tapped his shoulder.

Garry whipped around, hand on his gunbutt. 'Ben Gault, you shouldn't do that.'

'Just wanted to renew our acquaintanceship.'

'Tapping a man on the shoulder can be dangerous.'

'Killing men is even more risky,' smiled the young man.

Garry Maine looked him over. The fawn suit was well tailored, but a jacket didn't entirely conceal the Colt Peacemaker in its new holster.

'You pop up here and there,' Garry said. 'I'm wonderin' if I met you some other place besides Cedar Springs.'

'We met in the Gold Cougar – remember?'

'Where you went to play cards, but didn't.'

'I asked you at the time if you cared to share a drink with me. I'm asking again.'

'I've got to refuse. I'm on my way to see two old pals.'

'The girl seems to hate you.'

'You saw that ruckus?'

'Yeah. Behan's stepdaughter, isn't she?'

'What do you know about them?' Garry Maine threw a curious look at the other man.

'Just that you've killed the fellow,' came the calm reply. 'It isn't a secret, my dear man. Some T Bar T men are with the sheriff right now. I heard about it . . .'

Garry Maine gripped his arm. 'You hear lots of things. Like to tell me how much you've heard?'

'You've made a bit of a mess of things, Maine,' said the other man.

'So you know my name? I didn't give it to you the last time we met.'

'It isn't hard to get information if one digs hard enough. Sure, I know your name. I know lots of things. You tried to scare the hell out of

Mick Fulton that night. He's a pal of Behan's – that right? Or should I say – *was* a pal. I think you wanted to kill Fulton – that right, friend?'

'Maybe we'll have that drink pretty soon,' said Garry. 'But right now I've got to locate some men who are pretty important to me.'

'How are you going to placate Hec Shield? That should be mighty interesting. Or will you end up dangling on a hanging platform?'

Garry Maine removed the bandanna from around his neck. 'See those marks? Rope burns. My neck is still sore.'

'Interesting. How did it happen?'

Garry looked the other man over again, from head to foot, shrewdly. He said slowly, 'Some kind feller cut me down just before I was due to choke to death.'

'You seem to be a man destined for trouble, Mr Maine. I'd like to have that drink with you pretty soon – if you're not behind bars. I have a feeling you've had some eventful experiences.'

'You'd like to pump me?'

'I just feel a natural curiosity for interesting people,' Ben Gault chuckled.

'For a joker just in town on business, you ask a heck of a lot of questions.'

'I'm built that way. I'm really pretty harmless.'

'Like hell you are,' came the sharp reply. 'You

don't carry that smokepole for nothing, and you haven't once asked me why I killed Luke Behan.'

'They mistook you for a horse thief,' said Ben Gault. 'All you've got to do is prove you were simply an innocent rider attacked by a bunch of wild men.'

'Thanks for the tip. Waal, I'm on my way.'

Garry Maine had taken three steps along the boardwalk when Ben Gault called to him.

'I'd love to be present when you talk to Caleb Kray and Mick Fulton, but I don't suppose you'd invite me along.' Then Ben Gault walked off, smiling.

Garry stared. Who the hell are you, Ben Gault? What do you know about Kray and Fulton?

6

Depositions to a Sheriff

It was a strange meeting. Garry Maine felt like laughing at the enraged expressions on the faces of Caleb Kray and Mick Fulton. He had called at Kray's office and they had gone along to the Gold Cougar, where they had picked up Fulton and retreated to a small room upstairs.

Garry let them have it. 'You two will testify that Luke Behan threatened to kill me. If you don't, you'll have federal marshals making inquiries into your movements at Powder River City. Remember, I've done my time for stealin' that gold.'

'We could let you hang!' spat out Mick Fulton.

'The day I hanged, you two would be in the Pen. And maybe you'd get more than seven years.'

'Courts demand proof —' began Caleb Kray.

'I'll prove enough for you two to get sick just thinking about it,' said Garry. 'What I want is simple. You just make statements to Hec Shield. You say Behan wanted me dead.'

'Hec Shield will think the whole thing is mighty suspicious,' Caleb Kray said. He took out a silver cigar case, selected a thin cheroot and stuck it in his mouth. 'Why did Behan want you dead – that's what Hec Shield will want to know.'

'Just say something that's partly true – that he knew me years ago and we fought about money. Say Behan knew I was in town to look him up. When I went out to his ranch I was thrown in a cooler. Then, when I went back to see him at night, I was attacked by a bunch of riders with Behan in the lead. I had to defend myself . . .'

Mick Fulton couldn't stand still. He paced the room like a caged bear, rubbing his hands together. He whirled suddenly. 'You killed him! And you want to kill us! You must think we're fools, Maine – you want us to get you off the hook, then you'll turn on us when it suits you.'

Garry shrugged. 'All right, don't help me. Then the law will get you for that stolen Powder River Mine gold.' Garry Maine stuck his hands in his coat pockets and sauntered around the room. He laughed. 'Ain't you figured it out yet, Mick? You get me off the hook – and then it's you two and me. Heck, you can easily get that gunny onto me again . . .'

'Bart Logan?'

'That his name?' Garry looked at them with cold eyes. 'You hold a good hand, Mick. As a gambler you ought to see that. Clear me and you stand a good chance of hangin' on to what you've got. Don't, and you and Kray will surely hit the Pen.'

Mick Fulton went to Caleb Kray, his face working nervously. 'Can we do it? Is this the only way?'

The lawyer glanced at Garry. 'Unless you want to find a gun and stick it in Maine's ribs right now, I suggest that we cooperate . . .'

Garry grinned. 'You don't really want to play fool games right now, do you? I suggest you get your story together and go along to the sheriff's office, pronto.'

Caleb Kray nodded. 'All right. So we'll play it your way, Maine.'

Garry left the saloon building and walked carefully along the street. The old hatred he had nursed against Kray and Fulton had not diminished. He resented how they'd got away with the gold, and he couldn't forget that horrifying moment when it seemed he was about to die at the end of the rope. Hatred of these two still seethed in his guts. Maybe he should have killed them instead of taking part in this crazy game they were playing.

But of course that was the foolish way to deal with two double-crossing devils. That way he would really be a wanted man. But now, if Kray and Fulton talked hard enough, they would contradict the evidence of the T Bar T cowboys, and then Hec Shield would have to decide that the killing of Luke Behan was not murder.

It was ironic that Kray and Fulton were now forced to help him. And he knew that Kray, the lawyer, was smart enough to cook up a convincing tale.

Garry Maine decided to have a couple of slow drinks in some saloon – not the Gold Cougar – and kill some time. He'd know soon if Hec Shield intended to arrest him.

The saloon he chose was a rough-and-ready place where wide planks on huge barrels served as a bar counter. A cracked mirror behind the crude bar was heavily fly-specked. The bartender was a burly character in a leather apron. His balding bullet head jerked at Garry as he sidled to the bar.

'What's your poison?'

'I'll have a beer – if you've got a clean glass,' said Garry, surveying some used mugs standing in a bunch on the pine planks.

Garry got his glass of beer and raised it to his lips as he looked around at the customers in the place, only six men. One stood morosely at the bar and barely flicked Garry a glance. The others were at tables, three of them at one table playing poker. The two others sat singly. One, an old man, wore a black suit, string tie and a black derby hat. His garb and his thin face made him look like an undertaker without much business. Garry threw him an amused glance, then turned away. But seconds later he looked at the man again, thoughtfully. Where had he seen that long thin face before? The man's melancholy expression and thin, scholarly look seemed familiar.

Garry Maine pondered for some time, contemplating his beer so intensely that the bullet-headed barkeep asked belligerently, 'Somethin' wrong, mister?'

'Not a thing. The beer is surprisingly good.' On an impulse then, Garry took his glass over to the table where the old fellow sat with his whisky. Garry sat down, the back of the chair in front of him. 'Howdy, friend. You must excuse me – but you remind me of somebody.'

'The feeling is not mutual,' said the man in the

derby. 'And by that I mean no offence. I'm afraid I don't know you, sir.'

Garry grinned in good humour. 'Sorry if I'm intruding, but I'm sure I've seen you somewhere before. Ever get that feeling, friend?'

'I believe it happens to most of us.'

'Care for a drink with me? My name's Garry Maine.'

The old fellow looked sadly at his nearly empty glass and made no comment. Garry went back to the bar, got a bottle of whisky, brought it back and filled the old man's glass. He took the bottle back and settled with the bartender who had distrust stamped into every deep line of his face. When Garry returned to the old fellow's table again, the man had taken off his black derby to expose thin grey hair.

'Kind of warm today,' said the man. 'I think this town is due for some hot days ahead. Spring is behind us now, don't you agree?'

Garry Maine knew one thing clearly at that moment: he had seen this man in prison. But he didn't let this show in his face. He smiled at the man. 'Yeah, it'll get real warm soon. You're new to this town, sir?'

'What makes you say that?'

'The way you talk about the weather . . .'

The man nodded. 'As a matter of fact, I've been

in Cedar Springs only a few days. Got off the stage three days ago . . .'

'You lookin' for a job?'

The wary eyes flicked just once. 'Yeah.'

Garry figured the man wasn't nearly as old as he looked. He said, 'What kind of work do you want? I might hear about somethin'.'

'I'm a clerk.'

'A bank or maybe somethin' in the freight line?'

'Just a clerk,' smiled the man and he sipped his drink.

'Well, who knows? I might learn of somethin' that will suit you,' said Garry. 'If I do, what name would I mention?'

'Ah, the name is Smith. William Smith.'

When Garry Maine left the man some minutes later, having failed to learn much more from him, he was sure 'Smith' was not the man's name.

Something nagged at Garry. Cedar Springs was a long way south of Butte. Odd that two men who'd been in the same penitentiary should wind up in Cedar Springs. Montana was wide and handsome, and a released prisoner could go to any point of the compass.

Maybe it was just one of those coincidences that most men encounter from time to time. Still, it would be interesting if his memory could dig up some details on the fellow.

He was still thinking about the thin man when he felt the pangs of hunger and decided to go to an eating-house. At the hotel he was paying only for his bed, and they didn't like his rough, stained clothes in their dining room. Garry found a place where he could eat steak and all the trimmings for a low tariff. He had to economise. Maybe he should have asked Kray and Fulton for money.

When Garry emerged into the street after his meal, the sun was high in a cloudless sky. He found himself wondering where Lucia Ward had gone. Had she come into town just to challenge him? Or had their meeting been coincidental?

He went along to the law office but didn't enter the brick building. Instead, he stationed himself on the other side of the street, seated on the boardwalk. He wanted to see if the lawman had any callers. But maybe Kray and Fulton had already made their visit with a convincing statement about Luke Behan.

Garry sat in the shade and wished he had a new hat. The old one had gone spinning off when Lucia Ward had hit him with the whip, and he hadn't seen it again. If he didn't watch it, he'd be classed as a town bum – that's if they didn't pick him up for murder.

He was sitting there ruminating, his long legs stuck out, when a man left the sheriff's office. He moved slowly, halting to light a cigarette he'd rolled.

Garry Maine saw the glint of a tin star on his shirt. He wore a leather vest that looked new. His fawn flat-topped hat showed no sign of rain and sun. He seemed to be about thirty-five. Garry felt sure this was Hec Shield, sheriff of Cedar Springs, and not a deputy.

Garry got up and walked straight over to the man. Keen grey eyes set in a lean, humorous face looked into his.

'I'm Garry Maine.'

The lawman blew out smoke. 'So you're the big man.'

'Do you want to talk to me?'

'Maybe. What have you got to say, Maine?'

'I killed Luke Behan in self-defence. He sent a bunch of riders gunning for me. Earlier that day his men threw me in a cooler, but I got out.'

'I've had two sets of statements made to me,' said Hec Shield, 'and they contradict each other. The T Bar T men say you were snoopin' around the ranch. They figured you for a horse thief, so 'hey went out with Behan to run you off the ｀anch. The other statement comes from two reputable local men – men who knew Behan – and they say he had a grudge against you. I refer to Mr Kray and Mr Fulton, who are well-known in this town.'

Garry smiled. 'That's real nice of those two gents – and it's true. Behan hated my guts.' That much he could say with confidence.

'Why did you ride around the T Bar T in the dark? Do that around any ranch in this territory and you're asking for grief, Mr Maine. They get their share of rustlers and horse thieves.'

'I just figured to tell Behan that I objected to the way his men threw me in that cooler.' Which was partly true.

The two men stared into each other's eyes for some moments. Garry saw a man who wouldn't be easily fooled. He knew he wasn't kidding the man to any extent. Hec Shield would pounce on him the moment he had proof. Only the statements of Caleb Kray and Mick Fulton had saved him.

'You're a free man, Mr Maine,' said Hec Shield. 'For the moment. But don't give me any further trouble.'

'Thanks.' Garry walked away, feeling strangely uneasy. As he'd talked to Hec Shield he'd had the crazy desire to explain, to justify himself. There was something straight and reliable about the sheriff. But how could he tell the sheriff about hatred that had pushed him on to a course of retribution that involved killing three men? All right, the unholy three had tricked him, had allowed the law to pick him up while they got away with gold worth a hundred thousand dollars. They had left him to rot in jail while they shared the loot three ways. They'd had three years to consolidate themselves in a new town, while he'd slaved in prison work parties or had stared through bars. Then had come the attempted hanging and the paid gunhandler.

Garry went away, a sour feeling clouding his mind. He was on the wrong side of the law and it would have to stay that way. He'd been on the lawless trail the moment he'd decided to work with Behan, Kray and Fulton and steal the gold.

It was still in his brain that Caleb Kray and Mick Fulton had to die. He had vowed to kill them.

He decided he needed a drink. The bustling town, where new buildings went up almost every week, was not short of saloons, but Garry felt it would be best to avoid the places likely to be patrolled by Hec Shield or a deputy. He walked out of town and down to the river where the roar of the rapids could be heard. Here were the two tent saloons he'd heard about.

Looking around inside the largest, he saw a wild bunch. Here were the real drifters of Cedar Springs, the hardcases, the gamblers, men without families or jobs, and some men who might be featured on Wanted bills in other States. A few ranch hands among them were watching a spinning roulette wheel. It was early in the day and the night's activities were yet to start in earnest, but the tent was almost full. An enormous fat man in a grey frock coat and a stovepipe hat seemed to be in charge of the tent. Cigar in mouth, he moved from the bar to the card tables and then to the wheel. Garry Maine watched him, noting the dangling holster, the belt around the big waist and the pin-striped trousers.

Then Garry realised he was being watched. Turning slowly, a mug of beer in his hand, he stared at two men. It was a moment or two before he realised one of the men was the fellow he'd jumped last night, the man with Luke Behan.

The man glared at Garry, and the ranch hand with him also seemed hostile. Maybe he had been one of the hands with Behan's group last night.

Garry waited, not wanting trouble. But he sent back a bland stare; he was damned if he'd look the other way.

The two men strolled over to the bar. Garry

turned slowly and faced them.

'You know me,' said Sam Roper.

'Maybe.'

'I'm the ramrod at the T Bar T. You damn near killed me last night when you jumped me . . .'

'Do you want me to apologise?' Garry drawled.

'A real ornery cuss,' the other man put in. 'Just like you said, Sam.'

'He killed Behan. And it seems the bastard has got away with it.'

'Damned if I know why,' said the second man. 'What's wrong with the law in this town?'

'Behan was a good boss to me,' said Sam Roper. 'I figured I was on the inside track with him – and then you came along and blasted him. Maybe Mrs Behan will sell the ranch. Maybe I'll lose my job.'

'You seem full of maybes, friend,' said Garry.

'The name is Sam Roper. We came to town to make depositions to the sheriff about you. You're a killer, Maine.'

'Well, at least you know my name.'

'Why'd you kill Behan?'

'He came for me with a gun and a bunch of armed riders.'

'That's a load of garbage! You were lookin' for him. And by God I won't forget the way you jumped me.'

Then Sam Roper lost his temper and tried to fling a punch at the tall man. The arm was blocked by a suddenly raised glass and beer spilled to the floor. Enraged, Sam Roper tried to ram home his left fist. Again it was parried by the glass. At that point the other ranch hand took the view that he could demolish Garry Maine. He threw a punch that jarred against the big man's shoulder.

Before the brawl could develop any further, the fat man in the frockcoat appeared as if by magic, and with him was a huge man in a red shirt. Each held a gun.

'Out, you three! Get down to the river. All fights are on the river bank. House rule.' This came from the fat man whose mouth was full of brown, broken teeth.

'I don't want to fight,' Garry said.

'You got one. Now get to the riverbank – unless you can digest lead in your belly.'

It was ludicrous, but the fat man and his companion in the red shirt were two who apparently loved their rule book. In no time Garry and the two ranch hands were taken from the tent and pushed down to the grassy riverbank, a trip of only some twenty yards.

'Now you can kill each other,' said the fat man cheerfully.

'When you feel right peaceful, come back to the tent for medicine,' said the red shirted man huskily. 'We ain't sore. We've just got to be careful about the profits . . .'

'You heard the orders,' said Garry. 'All fights right here.'

Sam Roper and the other hand looked at each other.

'All right, let's get him,' said the ranch hand. 'His size don't matter. I've seen bigger galoots than him fold up.'

Garry smiled and began to unbuckle his gunbelt. But he kept a wary watch on the cowmen. As Garry's gunbelt hit the grass, they dropped their own rigs.

They circled Garry, then they jumped at him together, fists flailing. It was a barrage most men would have retreated from. But Garry hammered out with his long arms. He moved his arms like pistons. A right slammed into Sam Roper's face. A left went out and this time the other man's mouth took the jarring blow. Garry took two strides back and was clear of the barrage.

They hadn't touched his face yet. His height had helped in that respect. Their blows had thudded into his chest and it was like palm slapping a solid tree. Pretty soon Garry Maine knew they were not going to abide by the rules of the

Marquess of Queensberry. They kicked at him. One boot landed on his shin and he grimaced with pain. He sent a brutal blow at the man who had kicked him and felt it land like a hammer smashing into a hog's ribs. Then Garry jerked away, trying to avoid a blow that glanced off his head. Sam Roper crowded him, for the moment in a good position. His fist flashed out and rammed fair against Garry's mouth. Garry backed away and jabbed twice at Roper's cheek. Raging, Roper tried to repeat his big blow. He got near, then a hooking left from Garry hit him so hard between the eyes that he staggered around in a circle, blinded.

The other ranch hand wasn't without guts. He rushed in, got inside Garry's guard and landed a punch that rasped skin from Garry's cheek. Then the big man's arms wrapped around the hand, lifted him up and then flung him down at the ground.

The man lay still, momentarily stunned. Garry turned and waited for Sam Roper to shake the mists from his eyes and come back to fight. The ramrod stopped lurching about in his drunken orbit and came warily to his opponent. His fists rammed out when he judged the distance was right. Garry knocked one punch away but a fist came through and slammed on

the point of his chin. Garry balanced on the balls
of his feet and then let Roper have a savage right
that flattened his mouth and loosened teeth.
Roper teetered back and Garry went at him, his
big stride taking him close enough to land a
bone-cracking one-two. The fists followed each
other into Roper's eyes so fast it was like one
terrible mule kick. Roper went down to the
ground and huddled, moaning.

The other T Bar T man came back for more,
but he'd brought no real skill to the encounter.
He lashed out but Garry blocked, then delivered
the fast one-two. With the strength and weight
Garry Maine possessed, all conscious thought
left the man's brain and he fell limply to the
ground. Garry rubbed his knuckles and licked a
cut lip. But there wasn't much other damage. He
bent to pick up his gunbelt and strapped it on.
The two downed men didn't even stir.

Garry skirted the big tent and went back to
the main stem. He called in at the livery to see
that the black stallion was getting good treatment, then he went along to the hotel.

He hoped the supercilious desk clerk wouldn't
give him his disdainful scrutiny, as he had done
more than once. It was incredible, but the thin
little clerk annoyed him. He'd just dealt with two
tough men in a fight and he was allowing

himself to be rubbed the wrong way by a clerk!

Whistling, hands in his coat pockets, Garry walked past the man and went up the flight of stairs to his room. He turned the key and walked in – then froze.

There was a man in the dim room. He said:

'Reach or I'll kill you – right now!'

7

Mystery Men in the Night

Ben Gault knew he was acting illegally. He stood on the boardwalk, blessing the fact that the night was a perfect shroud for his activities. The nearest street lantern was some distance away. Caleb Kray's office was some distance from the saloons, which were the only areas of activity at this time of night. But he had to work quickly.

He tried three skeleton keys on the lock before one turned. The lock was an expensive new one, but he had keys for all products of the locksmith's trade. He pushed the door open.

There were two rooms inside the place, one of which was an outer office where presumably the clerks worked. The door to the inner sanctum was also locked, but Ben Gault had a key on his ring for that, too.

Inside the second office he stood for some moments looking at the desk, the green-leather chairs, the old-fashioned safe. Well, he also had a key for that.

A smile played about Gault's lips as he thought of Garry Maine. That worthy was doing things the hard way. Trouble was, he'd killed a man who'd possessed a lot of secrets. If Maine killed the other two and it seemed that was his intention, then a lot of information would die with them.

But maybe the safe held some interesting papers. Caleb Kray was a shrewd lawyer, but lawyers had one weakness; they liked to see details on paper.

Ben Gault tried the drawers in the desk and found two that were locked. He had small keys on his ring for these locks. It was hard to see in the darkness. He had matches, but he would chance striking a light only if he thought some books or papers merited attention. He went to work and opened the drawers.

As he had suspected, the papers he found were mainly connected with current deals and probably legitimate. He was looking for something else.

He had to turn to the safe eventually. He'd be satisfied to find only one clue. It was his opinion that all the gold stolen from the Powder River Mine had not been sold or banked, but had been hoarded somewhere by the three men, to be used when they needed extra capital to expand their businesses or to acquire property.

And Caleb Kray had been the brain behind the plan to hoard the gold rather than sell it all at once and so invite suspicion.

One man was dead. Of the two left, Kray undoubtedly held the key to the missing loot.

For about thirty minutes Ben Gault explored the safe and its contents, then he had a look through the desk again. He was careful to leave papers and ledgers just as he'd found them. No need to warn the man . . . that wasn't in the plan . . .

He did make a find in the safe, and this he transferred to his inner pocket, chuckling to himself. Even in the brief light of a match he'd seen enough in the little notebook to excite him.

Gault left then, closing the doors carefully. Nothing had been forced; he had done nothing that would raise a hue and cry. Ben Gault went into the dark street when he was satisfied there was nobody to see him. He walked quickly towards the lighter stretch of road, where a lantern cast yellow light on a corner. As he walked, a lithe, dandified figure in his fawn suit and new hat, he passed under the pool of lantern light. A good distance behind him, like part of the shadows in this backwater of a street, a thin man slipped from the doorway where he'd been hiding. He had observed the strange activities of the man ahead, and he'd seen him clearly in the light cast by the corner street lamp. He would know him again.

The thin man in the black suit and round black derby slipped away, avoiding the light like a nocturnal animal. Then, in a busy street some minutes later, he stood outside the painted glass window of a saloon, an insignificant figure with a melancholy face. He was thinking about what he'd seen.

It seemed that Caleb Kray was attracting some attention from a man who looked like anything but a petty thief. But then, one never knew what a crook might look like. He'd met a few strange ones in his time . . .

He wished he could go into the noisy saloon for a drink and join in the companionable row that was going on, but he couldn't afford more than one shot.

But maybe the day was not too far off when he would collect on the chances that were coming his way. After all, he had always kept alert, even in the jail at Butte, an insignificant man made to seem even more so in his drab prison garb. But he had heard a lot . . . clues and facts . . . men who opened big mouths and talked . . . even men who talked in their sleep.

The man who had entered Caleb Kray's offices had had keys, strange. Keys weren't easy to obtain. Who the hell was the man?

The man who called himself William Smith shook his head as he glanced again at the batwing doors leading to the warmth and joviality of the saloon. He was thinking how strange it had been that he had chosen to watch the lawyer's office that night. He had wanted to look at the place, eye it in the shadow of darkness rather than the light of day. He had wanted to muse on the fact that this was the office where Kray, a rich man by his standards, worked and ran his affairs. It was an office he would walk into one day . . . in the daylight . . .

'Just keep your hands real high, Maine!'

At Bart Logan's warning, Garry Maine raised his hands high. He knew the gunman could have blasted him into a crumpled heap the moment he opened the door and stood outlined in the faint light from the passage lamp. Why hadn't he?

'Howdy, pal. We meet again,' drawled Garry. 'How's the leg?'

The man in black sat on the window sill opposite the door, a smile his only answer.

'You got yourself a new smokepole,' said the man at the wrong end of the gun. 'Out to earn more money?'

'You can quit the stupid talk,' said Bart Logan. 'Just turn around.'

'You gonna let me have it in the spine?'

'You know damn well I could have killed you a minute ago . . .'

'Why didn't you?'

'Turn, damn you!'

Garry Maine turned, slowly. While he lived there was hope. Bart Logan had some kind of plan or he'd have fired by now.

'Drop the gunbelt, Maine.'

Garry smiled ruefully. He had to obey. Even the swivel holster couldn't help him. It was a certainty that Logan's finger had been trembling on the trigger from the moment Garry had appeared in the doorway. He unbuckled and the gunbelt dropped. Garry waited.

'Who dug the lead out of your thigh? Was it Doc Saville? A smart little feller.'

'Just shut up. Kick that belt to one side.'

Garry obliged and resumed the banter.

'Guess the wound hurts, huh? Should've been your gun hand, old pal. How the hell did you get in here? The door was locked.'

Surprisingly, Bart Logan answered. 'There's a verandah below this window. The woodwork is as good as a ladder, even with a stiff leg.'

'Maybe we can talk terms? How much are they payin' you?'

'You're just a saddletramp, Maine,' snarled Logan. 'All you've got are the clothes you stand in and that big stallion. Now, open the door again.'

'What's the idea?'

'You know damn well a shot in here would attract attention and I'd have to get away quick. With my bad leg that's not so good. So we're going for a little walk. I'll kill you in some dark alley. That way I'll get clear and a dead man in an alley ain't unusual. You'll just be one more corpse bound for Boothill. Now start movin' – and remember I'll shoot if you try something.'

'You're very explicit,' said Garry mockingly. He opened the door, taking his time. But he didn't want Logan to lose his patience and decide to kill him there and then, so he moved out to the passage and towards the staircase.

'We've got an inquisitive little clerk behind a desk here,' said Garry. 'You've got to get past him – or should I have kept my trap shut on that point? No matter. It'll be interestin' to see how you do it.'

'Thanks for the tip.' Logan prodded Garry in the back with the gun. 'Get.'

They went down the stairs to the lobby. The clerk sat on a stool behind the counter, nodding wearily. His sleepy eyes barely flickered at the two men. All he saw was a man in black holding his hat in his fist.

In the street Garry Maine slowed his pace. He was in no hurry to make a rendezvous with death.

'You can turn left, mister,' sneered the voice behind him.

It was an alley, black as the inside of a coffin.

Garry wished he'd killed Logan when he had the chance. He turned obediently, knowing that if he went another yard he was dead.

He halted. 'Mind if I take off my coat, Logan?'

'Why?'

'I'm sweating, friend. Don't know why. Maybe I don't feel like dying . . .'

'You're scared,' said Logan with a sneer. In that moment Bart Logan lost his icy coolness. But not in anger. It was just a human desire to crow. 'Hell, I knew it – no man can walk to his death without feelin' his guts turn to water.'

'I – I – guess you're right. It's too damn warm . . . don't know why . . . wasn't warm an hour ago . . .'

'Sweat, you big bastard!' gloated Bart Logan. 'I ain't seen a dead man sweat afore.' He laughed.

'Just let me take off my coat,' Garry pleaded. Halted, his broad back to the gunman, he looked a helpless target.

'So you're yellow-livered after all,' jeered Logan. 'You're just so much meat —'

'Can I take this coat off? It's warm, I tell you.'

'All right, take it off. You'll die just the same . . .' Garry began to slip out of the sheepskin coat. He made the customary movements of a man shedding a garment, knowing the gun was right behind him and would snarl out a slug as fast as the trigger finger could react. He had to beat that reaction.

It was his last chance. He had to move like a mountain cat, commanding speed that was beyond the ordinary. If he failed, he was finished.

The coat slid from his arms. He let it dangle in one hand for a fraction of a second, then the garment was swinging back and Garry was diving for the ground. The coat flew at Bart Logan's gun hand.

The killer had been off-guard for just a moment, but he fired his gun the moment Garry Maine flung the coat. The sheepskin hit the gun as the Colt spoke. The slug was deflected and the weight of the coat made Logan's hand dip.

In that breath-taking moment of deliverance, Garry Maine grabbed at Logan's ankles. Then he tugged hard and Bart Logan toppled back, his spine ramming against the alley floor. Retaining his grip on his gun, he tried to throw off the sheepskin coat that had been the cause of all the trouble. But he was given no chance to bring his gun into play again. Garry Maine transferred his hands from the man's ankles to his gun arm. He brought the man's forearm down hard on his knee. He heard a brittle sound of bone cracking and a yelp of agony. The gun fell. Logan's right arm was broken.

That might have been the end of the fight, but Garry Maine was swept along by his fury. He swept aside his coat, grabbed at Bart Logan's throat and, getting to his feet, hauled the man up. Glaring eyes, rolling in pain and shock, met his. Garry thrust the man away in disgust. But his whole body was tuned to extraordinary physical effort and the thrust was more of a ramming push to the earth than anything else. The gunman thudded to the ground. His head jerked to the side like something on a broken puppet. When Garry Maine bent down to examine the man, he knew he was dead.

Logan's neck had broken.

Drawing in the cool night air, Garry stared. He took one more look and felt for a heartbeat. There was none. Garry Maine picked up his coat and walked away. The shadows took him. No one had walked past the alley; no witness had been in the street either on foot or horseback. He returned to the hotel, putting his sheepskin coat on just before he walked into the light of the lobby. As he did, he saw the burn mark and the hole in the material from Logan's bullet.

The clerk was half asleep on his stool. Garry walked upstairs and went into his room.

Early the next morning the body was discovered and taken to the mortuary behind Doc Saville's place, then the sheriff was informed. As far as Hec Shield could see, there were no clues except the Colt that had been fired once. Doc Saville told him that the dead man had been to him for treatment. He'd taken a bullet in the thigh. The man wouldn't say how he'd got the wound.

Two men who received the news of Bart Logan's death were far from pleased.

They met in secret, as they seemed fated to meet these last few days, in a room in the Gold Cougar.

'Must have been Maine,' said Caleb Kray.

'Let's tell the sheriff.'

'Don't be a fool. Do you want questions asked?'

'That's right,' said Mick Fulton. 'Yeah, we had nothin' to do with Logan. Sure. But —'

'He's dead,' said the lawyer. 'That leaves us without protection. Maine is a savage. We – we'll have to deal with him . . . ourselves.'

'There are always guns for hire,' said Mick Fulton.

'I know. But if we kill Maine, then it's all over.'

'We tried that once when we strung him up. The snake had the devil's own luck. Somebody must've cut him down. That's been a real puzzle to me.' Mick Fulton reached out for the whisky bottle, his hand shaky. 'How the hell can we kill him, Kray?'

'By tricking him. Maybe if we sent him an anonymous message . . . about gold waiting for him . . . his share of the loot . . . we might get him out of town . . .' Caleb Kray's hawk-like face went vicious. 'A body can be buried out in the wilds so that even a coyote wouldn't find it . . .'

8

Grim Rendezvous

Garry Maine spent a lot of time that morning on Main Street. Not that the activities of the town interested him – he was watching for reactions from Caleb Kray and Mick Fulton. He stood outside the Gold Cougar for a time, then he went along to look at Kray's office.

He told himself he had to kill them. They had lived too long. He had to force out his smouldering hatred. He did his best to create impatience in his heart and mind, reminding himself that Behan had died and the other two had to follow.

After hours of this waiting game, he saw the little man in the black derby hat. Garry halted abruptly when he saw the man stop outside Kray's office. He watched as the thin man looked up at the falsefront of the building and then, apparently making up his mind, opened the solid door.

The man known as William Smith was inside the office for about thirty minutes. When he came out, his pale face was flushed. Garry stepped in front of him and saw the excited glitter in his eyes.

'You been consultin' your lawyer, friend?' Garry asked, searching for tell-tale reactions in the man's face.

'Ah, Mr Maine. You —'

'How come you need a lawyer? You've been in town only a few days, you told me. Did you see Kray?'

'Ah, yes, as a matter of fact.'

'A shrewd galoot, ain't he?' said Garry. 'But what kind of business would a man like you be having with a lawyer?'

'Isn't that my affair?' The man tried to side-step Garry but was blocked.

'You don't look like you need legal advice,' said Garry. 'You're fresh from the Pen at Butte.'

'You – know that?'

'I can't place you or remember your real name, if I ever knew it, but you know me. I saw it in your eyes when we met in the saloon, but you tried to pretend you'd never seen me.'

'You're making a mistake,' said William Smith,

recovering his composure. 'You have got me confused with someone else, sir.'

With that, Smith managed to slip to the side of Garry. He walked rapidly down the boardwalk. Garry watched him go, wondering why he couldn't place him. Well, most men in prison are only faces; the clothes made men look alike.

Maybe he could hammer the information out of Caleb Kray. On the other hand, if Kray died, then William Smith's business with him would die, too – unless he had actually needed legal advice from him.

It was just ten minutes after the little man with the melancholy face had disappeared that Caleb Kray came out of his premises and hurried along to the Gold Cougar. Garry watched him, pressing back into a doorway. The man had not seen him.

'Goin' to see your pal, huh?' Garry mused as he eased into the street again. 'And in a damn hurry.'

Minutes after Caleb Kray had vanished into the ornate building, Garry Maine watched and wondered. He wished he knew what it was all about.

The tedious business of waiting came to a halt when Garry saw Caleb Kray and Mick Fulton leave the false-fronted Gold Cougar. Bulges in their long jackets suggested gunbelts. Hurrying, the two men went around the gable end of the building. After about fifteen minutes they came back into sight, riding two good chestnuts. Evidently there was a livery behind the Gold Cougar. They cantered down the main stem for only a few dozen yards and then turned off at the Mercantile Bank, moving along an alley. Obviously they didn't want to be seen any more than could be helped. Garry decided to get his big black. When he rode out of the livery, which was situated near his hotel, he decided to track the two men and to keep himself out of sight.

A rise of the ground just out of the town enabled him to note that the two men had taken the western trail. He had noted, when the men had left the Gold Cougar, that they had rifles in the saddle holsters. Well, he had his own Winchester scabbarded, too. What was stirring his mind was whether he could push the two men into a fight. Maybe he could confront them farther out. As it was, they were heading in the direction of the T Bar T spread, proceeding leisurely at a half-walking gait. Had they business at the ranch or had something else taken them out so abruptly from Cedar Springs? Well, he'd soon find out. One intriguing point was the fact that Kray had got moving very soon after

William Smith had left his place.

Among Garry's few possessions was a spyglass. He had bought it in Butte just after being released. It had been one of his first purchases with the money the governor of the Penitentiary had given him. Now it was proving useful. He was able to make spot checks on the progress of the two men without getting too close.

Soon they left the stage trail and headed up the first slope of the hill known as Pike's Mount. The land was open range and the little hollows held bunches of cattle. At the top of the great hill pines grew in a thick barrier. They were about seven miles out of Cedar Springs and climbing the rising land, but they were now at an angle from the T Bar T area. It seemed they wouldn't go to the ranch after all.

After climbing steeply, the two men came to a log cabin which stood near a bubbling spring.

Garry Maine, still a long way behind, halted in the cover of a thicket when the two men dismounted. He used his spyglass on them and saw them take the rifles inside the shack. The door closed and there was no movement except for the two horses nosing at tufts of grass.

As Garry sat his horse, out of view of the men in the cabin because of the dense thicket, he

could hear the distant thud of axes on tree boles
and yells as men worked teams of log-dragging
horses. Miles back, hidden by the folds of numer-
ous valleys, lay Cedar Springs.

Garry waited and wondered. Several times he
wondered if he should ride up to the cabin and
call out to Kray and Fulton. This was the ideal
spot for a shoot-out, with no witnesses.

But it seemed now that the men were waiting
for someone. After more than a half-hour of waiting, Garry saw movement down the slope of
Pike's Mount. A small black dot had caught his
eye. Turning, he shoved the horse farther into
the thicket and put the spyglass to his eye again.

The figure on the slow-moving horse came into
focus. William Smith!

Garry watched the horse struggle up the hill,
ridden awkwardly, obviously a hired hack. He
couldn't guess what kind of business Smith
might have with Kray and Fulton. Whatever it
was, why had it to be conducted out here, miles
from anywhere?

The man in the round derby hat went past
Garry and rode to the log cabin. When the door
opened and a man stood framed in the opening,
Smith waved a greeting. Then he tethered his
horse with the other two and he and the man
entered the shack.

'A little get-together,' Garry muttered. 'A man from prison and two *hombres* who should have done seven years . . .

He wanted Kray and Fulton dead, but he also wanted to know what they had to discuss with the sad-looking Mr Smith. There was only one way to find out. He left his stallion tethered in the thicket, the rifle still in the scabbard, and he began to run up the slope.

Swiftly, like an Indian runner, he moved towards the shack, hoping to reach it without being seen. As he got close, he slipped his hand-gun from leather. His feet touched the springy, grassy earth with a minimum of sound. He came to a stop flat against the wall of the cabin, near a small window. The glass was dirty with years of neglect and one pane was cracked. He figured he hadn't been observed. He waited, drawing in breaths after his run. Then he grinned as he heard a murmur of voices. Maybe he could hear what was being said. He drew himself up to the window, his gun ready.

The three men were talking and he could hear most of the exchange when he got an ear close to the window.

'You think we're fools, Mr Smith?' sneered Mick Fulton. 'Why, we could blast you right where you stand.'

'Hold it, Mick,' said Caleb Kray. 'You know what we, ah, decided . . .'

'This third-rate jasper is tryin' to shake us for a share of the gold,' roared Mick Fulton. He was all confidence now; after all, the thin man didn't inspire fear.

'Well, it isn't much he's asking,' said Caleb Kray soothingly.

'He ain't entitled to a speck.'

'The gentleman has met us as requested,' said Kray placatingly. 'Maybe he'll tell us how much he knows – and, ah, who shares his information.'

'I know just enough,' came William Smith's quiet voice. 'I know you two men – along with Behan and Maine – took a small fortune from a wagon carrying refined gold from the Powder River Mine.'

'Now how did you get this highly fascinating news?' interrupted the lawyer in his silky voice. 'Details, Mr Smith, because we are really intrigued by your accusation. Tell us about the details . . .'

'There was a shipment of gold moving from the mine.'

'Look, we know what the hell went out on that wagon,' bawled Mick Fulton. 'I want to hear how it is you know all this. Just talk about that.'

'I was in the prison at Butte, with Maine.'

'Ah, he told you. But that's strange – Maine is usually tight-lipped.'

'He didn't tell me anything. I only saw him in the prison yard, and a few times out on a work detail. But I knew a man who shared a cell with Maine and two others . . .'

'Go on,' said Kray.

'I used to talk regular with this man in the exercise yard. He was a lifer – wouldn't get a release for about twenty years, and so the gold didn't mean a damn thing to him. But I was able to get him tobacco, and for this he talked to me – many times – in the yard, when the trusty wasn't looking. He told me about Garry Maine – the time when he was sick with fever for a whole week – and he talked in a delirium – day after day – and this man, this lifer, used to listen. Gradually, he pieced it all together – names – dates – the gold – his partners – it all came out as Maine tossed and turned.'

Garry flattened against the wall, realization hitting him. He'd been ill after about a year in the Penitentiary, and the authorities had given him no treatment. The head warder hadn't even sent for the prison doctor; he'd been left to suffer and either to live or die. The governor had never heard about it. Actually, Garry had forgotten bout that episode in his prison life.

119

'You evidently have a good ear for an interesting story,' said Caleb Kray smoothly. 'But you must admit the whole thing could be dismissed as a fabrication. You haven't one iota of proof.'

'I was told everything Maine babbled during his illness,' William Smith said. 'You wore full face masks made of silk. You took the gold from the wagon after you gagged and tied the guards. But Maine slipped and fell from the wagon. He banged his head on a wheel rim and was knocked out. You left him there.'

'Go on,' said Mick Fulton. 'What else?'

'The lifer pieced it all together. The three of you probably only figured to trick Maine out of his share of the gold. But while Maine was unconscious, one of the wagon guards got free of his ropes. He tied Maine up. Maine was tried, but he didn't talk. The guards knew there had been four men, but they couldn't describe the others because they'd been masked. Maine was sentenced to seven years. Three other men got away with a hundred thousand dollars in gold – and Maine never revealed their names.'

'The bastard wanted only revenge,' Kray said. 'He was willing to wait seven years, but luck was with him and he got a remission. We read about that in the newspaper – and we were waiting for him.'

'But you didn't kill him,' said William Smith. 'Well, that was your mistake. Anyhow, it's none of my concern. As I told you in the letter I had delivered to your office, Kray, I want a share of the loot. You two men can well afford it. You don't want the law to hear my story, do you?'

'We sure don't,' growled Mick Fulton.

'Then pay me off,' Smith said. 'You said you had the gold out here . . .'

Garry Maine stiffened against the cabin wall. He'd always thought that Behan, Kray and Fulton had kept some of the gold hidden. Gold could always be sold with no questions asked.

'Yes, we have gold,' was Kray's reply.

'But what makes you figure we'll hand over to you?' Fulton put in.

'You don't want the law —'

An angry snarl from Mick Fulton drowned the man's words. Garry Maine felt sure the two men were about to kill the ex-convict and got ready to make a move. But again Kray placated his friend. 'Now, look, Mick, we agreed to pay Mr Smith something – and he agreed to ride out of Cedar Springs and bother us no more . . .'

Mick Fulton mumbled incoherently and there were the sounds of boots on bare boards. Garry got the impression they were about to leave the cabin. This made sense. It wouldn't be smart to hide gold bars in the cabin, for drifters probably used the place.

Garry edged around the side of the cabin when he heard the door open. Were they going to pay Smith off? If so, he wanted to see where they were going. He decided to stay out of sight a bit longer.

He watched them mount their horses and start to ride higher up the slope. When they were out of sight behind a stand of pine, he sprinted back to the thicket for his own mount. Hitting the saddle, he nudged the black out.

Smith was playing with his life by blackmailing these two. Maybe his stay in prison had addled his brain. He should have insisted on a payoff in town.

The hillside the men were making for was studded with bits of rock. Garry watched the distant black shapes, wondering about the intentions of Kray and Fulton.

Garry rode around the lower part of the hill when the three men were hidden from view by rocky outcrops. He had to get them in sight again. He had to know what kind of trick Kray and Fulton were planning.

He tethered the stallion to a clump of brush and went up the slope on foot, gun in hand. He saw the three men suddenly and ducked out of sight behind a boulder. They had dismounted and were standing near a cliff face, looking up at what seemed to be a cave mouth.

Garry Maine couldn't hear what was being said. Fulton was pointing to the cave mouth and Kray was smiling.

Garry took a chance and ran towards the cover of another boulder, crouched low. He wasn't seen. Now he could hear what was being said.

'That's where the gold is . . .' This came from Caleb Kray.

Garry Maine knew at that moment that the two men meant to kill the ex-convict. And maybe Smith had the same feeling, for there was a quaver to his voice as he said:

'Let's settle right now. Pay me and I'll forget all I ever knew about Maine and you men and the gold.'

'You're a goddamn liar!' said Mick Fulton. 'There's one thing we know about blackmailers – they always come back for more.'

Mick Fulton was standing on a hump of ground just above Smith. Suddenly he bent and picked up a large rock and held it poised above the head of the ex-convict.

William Smith started to move but he was too slow. The rock came crashing down on his head. The black derby toppled to the ground as the rock cracked open his skull. He fell, blood gushing from his head. Then Mick Fulton picked up another piece of rock and rammed it down on the dying man. Then Kray kicked Smith in the head twice before he walked away. Mick Fulton glared down at the body.

'That should do,' Kray said.

'Little bastard tryin' to blackmail us!' raged Mick Fulton.

Kray sighed. 'He's dead – finished. Come on, we'd better get away from here.'

'One more rock,' Fulton said. 'I want to be sure of this little bastard.'

Garry Maine could stand no more of it. He came running from the cover of the boulder, gun at the ready. He wanted to get just a little closer and then he would fire.

But they heard him and whipped around. Then they hauled out their guns. But they were slow in drawing and this enabled Garry to cover valuable ground with his long strides before they fired. Their' bullets whined past him. Garry dropped to one knee and aimed. His gun bucked and the slug took Mick Fulton between the eyes.

Fulton fell like a rag doll from the hummock of earth. Garry Maine didn't get a chance to shoot at Caleb Kray. The lawyer ran, crouched low. Garry pounded after him, but then his right boot was wedged between two jutting rocks that were as good as a trap. He fell forward and hit the ground hard. His gun flew from his hand and he lay still. Caleb Kray didn't even look behind. He grabbed at his horse and vaulted to the saddle, then rode out from under the cliff face and heeled at his horse desperately.

9

Interrogation

Garry Maine had pushed himself up and was shaking his head to clear the fog that shrouded his brain when he heard the sound of an approaching horse. He flattened and looked around for his gun. It was on the ground some yards away. He was about to leap for the gun when the sound of hoofs became louder.

There was more than one rider. He sank back, then a man and a woman hauled in their horses and stared down at three sprawled bodies. One had a crushed head, another had been shot between the eyes – and the third moved.

The girl stared. 'It's Garry Maine – and he isn't dead.'

Sam Roper drew his handgun and scowled as he jigged his horse closer. 'God, it's Mick Fulton – deader than hell.'

Garry Maine got to his feet. The effects of the concussion had faded. He looked deep into the eyes of the tall blonde girl. 'We always seem to meet in strange circumstances,' he said. He bent to pick up his gun and when it was in his hand he turned to see Sam Roper covering him with his Colt. 'You got somethin' on your mind, friend?'

'Yeah, plenty. I figure you killed Fulton.' Roper waved his Colt. 'I want you to drop that gun, mister.'

'Maybe you'd like to hear what happened?'

'Drop that blasted gun!'

Garry smiled at the girl and angled his gun at the ground. 'Mick Fulton killed that little fellow, Lucia. He and Kray lured him out here and Fulton smashed in his skull. I was too late to stop it . . .'

She was bewildered. 'But why? Mr Kray and Mick Fulton were Luke's friends. And you killed Luke. Now Fulton is dead.'

'Don't you remember me telling you that Behan bought that ranch with stolen gold? It was when you drove your gig into Main Street and used your horse-whip on me. Well, Mick Fulton got his saloon the same way. And Kray also has stolen gold behind his success. This old fellow lying there with the smashed skull knew about it. They killed him and I killed Fulton.' His tone hardened. 'I'm going to kill Kray, too.'

'How do you know about this stolen gold?' she asked.

'Well, I was with —'

But Roper cut in, 'You don't fool me, mister! You're a killer. First Behan, now Fulton. Well, I guess the sheriff won't be fooled this time. I say drop that gun.'

Garry Maine looked into the man's bruised and swollen face and knew he was still incensed over the punishment he'd taken during their fight.

'I intend to go for my horse and ride after Kray,' Garry said easily.

'You're goin' to town to see the sheriff,' snarled Sam Roper. 'You can go healthy or slung over a saddle – your decision.'

Garry looked at Lucia. 'Tell him to try and see reason. He doesn't hold any cards in this play.'

Uncertain, she shot a look at the T Bar T ramrod. 'Sam, we don't want trouble. We're on our way to see Joe Swann at the lumber camp, remember? He wants to buy the ranch as soon as Luke's Will is read.'

'This *hombre* murdered Mick Fulton,' said the ramrod. 'He killed Behan and got away with it, but I'm damned if I know how. Well, he won't get away with this one.'

'You're wastin' my time,' Garry clipped out. 'I want Kray. Put that hogleg to leather, mister. I'm going for my horse.'

Garry Maine turned on his heel – but not before he saw a flicker in Roper's eyes. Garry's right hand went down and he whirled to face Roper.

Two guns roared. But Garry Maine's Colt was the first to fire. He beat the other man's trigger with a gun that whipped up in a flash. His gun sent a slug into the man's arm almost as Roper's gun exploded.

Roper's slug went wide by inches, then he jerked back in pain and dropped his gun, his left hand grabbing at the wound. His horse pranced, colliding with Lucia Ward's mount.

Garry didn't give Roper time to recover. He jumped at the cowman's horse as Roper fought to stay in the saddle. Garry pulled Roper's rifle from its saddle scabbard. Then he raised his handgun.

'You've lost out again, Roper. I reckon you'd best take yourself back to the T Bar T and get that wound attended to. I knew a feller who had his arm cut off because of lead poisoning. Well, you going?'

'Do as he says,' Lucia ordered. 'I'll ride part of the way with Mr Maine. I'd like to hear his story. Then I think I'll head for Cedar Springs and see that the sheriff gets out here before buzzards and timber wolves find these bodies.'

Cursing under his breath, Roper rode off.

Garry took Roper's rifle to his tethered stallion and rammed the rifle beside his Winchester in the scabbard. Lucia Ward sat her horse, looking down at Garry.

'You're going to kill Caleb Kray?' she said.

'Yes.'

'Tell me exactly why.'

'I haven't got the time.' He vaulted into the saddle and looked at her. 'How can I explain to you how it felt to spend three years hating three men . . . hating them so much I was poisoned by it . . . three years in a jail, Lucia.'

Suddenly there was warmth in her eyes. 'Killing Caleb Kray won't do you any good. Did killing Luke Behan achieve anything?'

'Not really . . .'

'And Mick Fulton?'

131

'He'd just murdered a defenceless man . . .'

'But you wanted to kill him anyhow.'

'He was one of the three who had to die . . .'

'You caused my mother a lot of heartache.'

He nodded. Eyes narrowed as he stared at the horizon, he felt restless. Kray was getting away from him. Maybe the man was heading for Cedar Springs, maybe not. He had to know, and in the meantime the girl was detaining him. He said, 'Somebody always gets hurt. I'm sorry about your mother – and about you. Maybe you ought to know that Behan and his partners tried to hang me. They caught me on the trail a long way out from Cedar Springs and they strung me up. Look!' He loosened his bandanna to show her the still purple bruises. 'I'd be dead if it wasn't for some stranger who cut me down.'

She sensed his impatience. 'I don't suppose you'd listen to me if I told you to forget about Caleb Kray . . .'

'Nope. I'm goin' . . .'

He wheeled the big black horse around and said: 'I'd like us to have a long talk pretty soon.'

Her bitterness came back. 'For that you'll have to stay alive, Garry Maine.'

'I intend to.' He waved to the girl. As he rode down the slope, he decided that this parting was not going to be final.

Garry Maine rode around in a wide loop, searching for a sign of Kray. Finally he saw him as a small dot in the distance. Kray was heading back to town. With the head start he'd gained, there was no hope of the big stallion catching up.

Somewhere behind, the girl was coming down from Pike's Mount. She'd said she'd inform the sheriff about the bodies on the hill. Garry wondered for a moment if he should go back and ride with her to town. Then the old restless bug about Caleb Kray nagged at him; he had to go on with it.

Garry cantered the black into town and saw Kray's horse tethered outside the sheriff's office.

So the lawyer had called on the sheriff. What sort of statement was he making? With his shrewd brain and legal training, he would be cooking up something to protect his own hide, that was for sure.

Making a bold decision, Garry decided to horn in on the party. He rode the black to the tierail, vaulted from the saddle, threw the reins around the bar in a swift loop and then he strode into the office.

Kray was totally surprised to see Garry. Even hatless he towered over Caleb Kray and the sheriff as he stood there, feet wide apart, a challenge in his eyes.

But it was the fast-moving brain of Caleb Kray that got in the first shot. 'That's him, lawman. He killed Mick Fulton and another man up in the hills – a stranger. As I was telling you, I got here as fast as I could.'

'You're a liar, Kray,' Garry said calmly.

Hec Shield raised a hand. 'Now, look, I want only the facts – and I'm not forgettin', Maine, that you killed Luke Behan in pretty strange circumstances. Now you first, Mr Kray.'

'It's simple.' Caleb Kray pointed a finger at Garry. 'This man murdered Mick Fulton and that stranger. He was obviously trailing us in the hills.'

'Why?' asked Hec Shield.

'He's a thieving, murdering skunk. He killed Luke Behan.'

'And you supported his argument that Behan was gunning for him.'

'Well, that was true to a certain extent.' Even Kray's quick mind was floundering now. 'I was just trying to be fair . . .'

Hec Shield hitched up his gunbelt and paced his office. 'I know that Maine entered the Gold

134

Cougar one night and tried to get Fulton to go for his gun. I got the story from some of the men who were there. So it seems that Maine was after Fulton's blood. The question I'd like answered by one of you two gents is why Maine wanted Mick Fulton to die.'

'I don't know,' rasped Caleb Kray.

Hec Shield swung to Garry. 'You ought to know, feller.'

Garry grinned. 'Mick Fulton didn't take my challenge that night, so there's no charge to answer.'

'I'd still like to know why you wanted him dead.'

'Private feud, Sheriff. Ain't unusual in these parts, is it?'

'I see. But he's apparently dead now – and Mr Kray says you killed him. But you've just called him a liar.'

'That's right. I didn't kill that stranger up in the hills. Kray and Fulton did that.'

A snarl of rage came from the lawyer.

'Go on, Maine,' the sheriff said.

'I killed Mick Fulton, but it was in self-defence. I'd just seen him murder the stranger by smashing his skull in with rocks. I went gunning for 'em. I figure I had the right of a citizen who'd just seen murder. I dropped

135

Fulton and maybe I'd've dropped Kray, too, but I tripped and hit my head on something, then Kray ran off.'

'Any witness?' asked the sheriff.

'Not that I know about,' said Garry. 'After I came to, Miss Lucia Ward and the foreman of the T Bar T rode up and we had a confab. She intended to ride in here and report to you, Sheriff, about the bodies, but I guess she rides a lot slower than I do.'

Hec Shield threw grim looks at Caleb Kray and then at Garry. 'All right, so you each accuse the other. You, Kray, say that Maine killed Fulton. He admits that, but he contends that it was self-defence. You, Maine, say that Kray and Fulton killed this other man. Have I got it right?' He paused. 'After all, I'm just a dumb lawman and I listen to an awful lot of lies.'

Garry said, 'You've got it all right, Sheriff. Kray and Fulton killed that stranger and I shot Fulton.'

'He killed Fulton and the other man,' Caleb Kray threw in. 'I've told you, Sheriff. Why don't you accept my story and throw Maine in jail?'

'Maybe somebody will see the inside of my hoosegow when I find out why that stranger had to be killed,' said Hec Shield. 'Who is this stranger? Why was he killed? You first, Maine.'

'I had no reason to kill him,' Garry said.

'And you, Kray?' Hec Shield said to the lawyer.

'I didn't know the identity of the stranger,' said Caleb Kray smoothly, 'and Fulton and I had no desire or reason to kill him.'

'Tell me one thing: why were you and Fulton up in the hills?'

'Business interests, Sheriff. We thought we'd visit the lumber camp.'

'If Maine here killed the stranger and Fulton, how come you got away?'

'Well, as he said, he tripped and I rode off. I thought the law could best handle Maine. I hope I'm not mistaken.'

'And you, Maine – why were you up on that hill?'

'Just ridin' around.'

Hec Shield sat down at his desk, his lean face taut. 'I'm bein' fed a pack of lies. According to both of you, there are two dead men halfway up Pike's Mount. Maine admits to killing Fulton but you accuse each other about the stranger. Well, I'm gonna find out the truth. I don't like unexplained dead men in my territory. We found one the other day – a feller by the name of Bart Logan. I've got some theories about him.'

He shot Garry Maine and Kray a keen glance. 'Don't leave town, gents. If you do, you'll be followed.'

'Aren't you going to charge Maine?' asked Caleb Kray.

'Not yet. Get out of my office, both of you. I'm leavin' a note for Pete Lowe, my deputy, and then I'm riding out to Pike's Mount.'

On the boardwalk steps outside, Garry saw the girl again. She reined in her horse, surprised to see him standing there. Then she saw Caleb Kray walk out of the office. 'You're still alive!'

He smiled coldly. 'You've been talking to Maine. Well, remember what he did to your stepfather, young lady. He's a killer through and through.'

'And you, Mr Kray? What are you?'

Garry's voice broke in. 'He's a dirty, crawling specimen trying to figure out some way to smash me. But he won't succeed.'

Kray snarled. 'You'll die, you fool. Soon – pretty soon.'

As Kray led his horse away, Garry Maine saw Ben Gault on the other side of the road. The dapper young man waved. He seemed quite cheerful. Garry wondered why the fellow was always around.

When Garry rode away with the girl, Ben Gault entered the sheriff's office and smiled at the lawman.

10

Secret of the Cave

'You say you spent three years in jail? For stealing gold? That makes you a crook.' Lucia's blue eyes were cold.

Garry nodded. 'I should have done seven years but I did a good turn for the prison governor. He got me a remission and gave me some money, most of which is gone.' Garry and the girl were seated at a table in a small restaurant, he an awkward big figure and she a pretty girl in blue jeans and a checked shirt. She could handle a tiny teacup with practised charm. He fumbled with the cup, finding tea a strange drink after the strong black coffee he usually drank.

'I was a fool,' he admitted. 'A young fool. Behan,

Kray and Fulton were older than me and I let them talk me into it. But I make no excuses for myself. We robbed the Powder River Mine of a hundred thousand dollars in refined gold. I went to prison and the other three lived the high life.'

It seemed natural to tell her the whole story. He told her about the way the three men had ridden away with the gold, leaving him unconscious. 'They thought I'd get away when I came around, but one of the guards got free of his ropes. I could have blabbed and got Kray, Behan and Fulton in the Pen with me, but by then I'd got the notion that only death was good enough for the skunks. So I poisoned myself with hate for three years, Lucia . . . hate nagging away inside me . . . changing me.'

'You've killed two of them. Why not leave it at that?'

'Will Kray leave it there?' he asked grimly.

'He might if you let him know you're through with your ideas of revenge.'

'I can't leave it unfinished.' The admission made him feel dirty somehow. 'Kray – walkin' around – rich – alive —'

'You say he and Mick Fulton killed that poor man. The sheriff might believe you.'

'Your sheriff hasn't any proof one way or the other,' he replied. 'He'll just have bodies.'

'Garry Maine,' she said gently, 'you're in big trouble . . .'

He grinned. 'And you Lucia Ward, are a mighty pretty girl.'

She returned his smile. 'I've had a few tell me that, and some were real gentlemen.' She sighed. 'But that kind are always a lot older than me.'

'I'm about eight years older than you are, Lucia . . .'

'Sure, but you don't wear a fancy vest and have greying hair.'

It was a pleasant way to pass the time; he and a tall, lovely girl in this little cafe. He could feel her charm creeping over him. Suddenly he felt trail-grubby and shabby in his old sheepskin coat. It struck him that he must compare badly with some of the men she had known. The thought did nothing for his self-esteem.

He told her a lot more; about the man known as William Smith and how he had died. Then he told her how he'd killed Bart Logan.

'Don't say anything to the sheriff as yet,' he said. 'In fact, keep it all to yourself.'

'It will come out eventually,' she warned.

'Maybe. But right now it isn't settled. There's still Kray . . .'

'You don't have to kill him. Ride out of Cedar Springs – forget it.'

'That way Kray wins. He's got gold hidden away – and I've got a hunch I know where it is . . .'

'Forget that too, Garry. The gold doesn't belong to you or Kray. I think you ought to tell the sheriff about that part of the story.'

'Yeah, the authorities would sure like to get some of that gold back. They questioned me plenty about it.'

'But you kept a tight mouth,' she said.

'I did. The mining company offered a reward for information leading to the recovery of the gold, but they got nowhere.'

Reluctantly, he had to part company with the girl. She had to ride back to her mother at the ranch. He saw her to the perimeter of town, tempted to go to the T Bar T with her. But the prospect of facing Mrs Behan was a bit daunting.

In any case the day was wearing to a close. He was on Main Street when Hec Shield guided a slow-moving horse into town, with another animal trailing behind on a lead rope. On the second horse's back were two bodies. One had a smashed skull and the other man had died with a bullet between his eyes. People in the street stopped to stare as the lawman took the horse and its burden to the mortuary.

That night Hec Shield called on Garry in the

144

hotel. Garry lay back on his bed, fully clothed, his gun in his hand.

'You can put that away,' said the sheriff. He paused. 'It seems Mick Fulton was killed with a handgun and the other man had his skull smashed by rocks.'

'And?'

'There was blood all over Fulton's boots and trousers.'

'So?'

'I think he got the blood when he rammed the rocks down on the stranger's head. How else would he get blood all over his pants?'

'A good question, Sheriff. Well, I told you who killed the little guy. It was Fulton and Kray. And I shot Fulton.'

'Yeah, but you didn't tell me why the little man was killed. And you knew he was straight from the Penitentiary at Butte – like you, Maine, an ex-convict. You knew that.'

Garry sat up. 'Who told you so, Sheriff? How did you know I'd been in prison?'

Hec Shield's smile was derisive. 'Just say I've got sources of information, Maine. I know why you were in Butte Penitentiary and why you were released.'

'How long have you known it?'

'Maybe I'll keep that to myself. I'd just like your

opinion as to why the other ex-con was killed.'

'Ask Caleb Kray. He helped kill him.'

The sheriff nodded. 'That man was murdered –
and some jasper is going to pay for it.' He moved
back to the bedroom door and paused. 'You got
away with the shootin' of Behan and I guess you'll
get away with the killing of Mick Fulton because
he was a party to murder – but don't push your
luck too far.'

Garry lay back on his bed thinking for a long
time after the lawman had gone. His thoughts
had only one effect: his brain swirled with hatred
of Kray. Recollections of the months in the prison
flooded his mind and an image of Caleb Kray's
snarling face floated in his brain. Why should
the man get away with everything?

But maybe Hec Shield was right. Maybe he'd
got away with as much as he could. One thing
was certain: the sheriff was getting his teeth
into this business, and maybe some day the
truth about three of Cedar Springs so-far
respected citizens would be made public.
Somehow the sheriff was getting important
information.

And then, along with his savage thoughts, he
had a vision of Lucia Ward telling him to forget
the gruesome game of kill or be killed. Maybe
she was right . . .

He lay for a long time, then realization leaped at him and he wondered why he hadn't seen it much sooner.

He jumped from the bed and looked down at the street. It was a typical night scene in Cedar Springs. Men on the streets were bound for a saloon. The day's work was over for most. But Garry was not really thinking about the activities of Cedar Springs; his mind was churning over the possible movements of one man.

His great hunch hammered at him; Kray might want him dead, but he would want something else above everything. Garry Maine knew there was no chance of further rest for him while this hunch prodded at him. He went around to the livery, taking his Winchester, his saddle-bags, blanket roll and few other possessions. The stallion neighed on seeing him and tossed his head. Garry saddled the animal, stuffed the rifle in the saddle scabbard, hooked the saddle-bag and bedroll in place and, with a wave to the old hostler, rode into the night and out of town.

If he was Caleb Kray, he'd be worried. There was the possibility of an accusation of murder. Cedar Springs might get too hot. In any case, now that Behan and Fulton were no more, there was one vital chore left.

Yeah . . . surely that was the way Caleb Kray would think. He was a shrewd man who never missed a trick . . .

Garry didn't know he was followed by another rider, a man who took great care to remain a long way behind his quarry but sufficiently close to get an occasional glimpse of his man in the moonlight. It was Ben Gault, clad in his immaculate fawn suit, his hat down over his forehead. and the Colt Peacemaker thonged tight against his thigh. Garry's well-rested horse worked willingly, and was surefooted on the dark slopes. Against the semi-purple sky the dark mass of Pike's Mount reared. Garry worked towards the spot where Fulton and William Smith had been killed. He saw the log cabin. As he skirted the place, the silence of the night pressed around him. The buzzing sawmill high on the mountain had ceased work; there was no sound of axes attacking the almost limitless timber. The lumber men would be in their shacks or in town, spending their hard earned money.

He rode to the cliff face where the men had died and stared up, but the cave mouth was lost in shadow. Clouds now obscured the moon.

He had to hide his horse. He looked around for a suitable place and found it around the corner of a rocky bluff. The cleft in the rocks was almost a natural stable, with over-hanging greenery that would hide the animal. He pushed the stallion into the place and hitched the leathers. Then he took his bedroll and rifle with him and began to climb the cliff face.

It wasn't hard to get handgrips, but chunks of weathered rock began to fall away as he climbed. They clattered to the base below.

He reached the cave mouth and crawled in. He put down his bedroll and rifle and began to look around. He had plenty of matches in his sheepskin coat pocket. Striking one, he moved away from the cave mouth.

The cave went back some distance. The roof was sometimes so low that he had to crouch. He looked for sign that men had been here – a box, canvas, food scraps, a candle – anything. But there wasn't a clue. Once or twice something scuttled before his crunching feet – a lizard, he thought, or maybe a rat. He struck four matches in his search but discovered nothing that excited him. As far as he could see, there had been no attempt at digging; nothing had been buried. He went right into the cave until the roof was only some two feet above the floor. He could progress no farther.

He returned to the cave mouth, peering into the darkness below, listening. His eyes were now adjusted to the darkness. If anyone approached he had a good chance of seeing him, and certainly if a man climbed the cliff face, he'd make plenty of noise.

He would play a waiting game. There might be no need for him to search. If his hunch was right, there'd be a man coming. If his hunch was wrong, events would shape differently.

He sat and thought about Caleb Kray again. The man dominated his mind; he began to brood. There was only one person who could change his brooding thoughts, and that was Lucia Ward. She was intruding now, images of her pushing the hate to one side. One moment he was soured with thoughts of Kray and the next he was filled with wonder as he remembered the beauty of this girl.

An hour went by, then another. He estimated it was long past midnight. Nothing stirred in the darkness below. But stubbornly he clung to his belief – and then he heard the sound of a horse. Listening and keeping well back, although the cave mouth was a patch of gloom, he realized there were two animals. Well, it figured.

Now that there was something on which to concentrate, he had the patience of an Indian, squatting, listening. He heard the movement of the horses cease. Muttered words came to his ears and then the sound of falling rocks. A man was climbing the cliff face. Garry Maine grinned; time to hide.

There was a deep cleft in the side of the cave, a slot just wide enough to take a man. He stepped into it, taking his bedroll and the rifle.

He was hidden when the approaching man showed as a dark shape in the cave mouth. Garry held his breath. The man went noisily along the cave, then stopped. There was the sound of a sulphur match being struck. Yellow light flared. Garry peered out.

It was Caleb Kray, as he had known. The man was a vague figure in a dark suit, hat firmly on his head, a gunbelt around his middle.

Kray had come for the remainder of the gold, Garry thought. *All right, Feller, show me where it's hidden.*

Kray moved deeper into the cave. He took about five crunching strides, stopped and lit another match.

So he and Fulton had not been fooling when they told William Smith the gold was here.

Caleb Kray suddenly bent and began to pull a slab of rock from the side of the cave wall. The slab was a neat fit. Kray had to work hard to free it. Then Garry heard his gasp of satisfaction and a moment later another match flared. Garry saw a steel box at Kray's feet. The box was from the bullion wagon. It would contain the small, easily handled gold bars.

Once again the match died, but Kray went on working. Evidently there were more boxes in the cavity.

Then Garry heard the sounds made by falling pieces of rock outside the cave mouth. Someone was climbing the cliff face. Another man! Did Kray have an accomplice? But no – Kray was silent now.

There was nothing else Garry could do but stay hidden in the cleft and wait for the arrival of this newcomer. Who else knew about this cave? Was it the sheriff?

Suddenly a man's figure appeared in the cave mouth. Garry, edging out, saw the lean, lithe shape and knew who it was – Ben Gault, the young fellow who seemed to be always around.

Garry caught his breath. Ben Gault was an easy target outlined in the cave mouth. In the flash of a second Garry knew what was going to happen.

'Down!' Garry cried.

Along with the warning came the roar of two guns in the cave. One gun belonged to Caleb Kray; the other was Garry's Colt .45. One shot was aimed at Ben Gault. The other bullet spat out of Garry's weapon, seeking the flesh of Caleb

Kray. But it was a wild shot.

One point favoured Ben Gault; Kray was not a good marksman and he had fired in a hurry, spurred on by sudden fear and the surprise of Garry's warning shout. So the slug whined past Ben Gault's face and went harmlessly into the night. Simultaneous with the gunplay came an ominous rumbling sound from deep in the cave. The vibrations set up by the guns had affected the rock roof.

There was the rumbling sound of crashing rock and then a terrible scream from Caleb Kray's throat that ended abruptly. Rocks tumbled into the end of the cave where Kray had stood and the gold was hidden. Garry, near the cave mouth, had jumped at the first ominous sound of breaking rock.

'It's me, Maine,' he said, then he was beside Ben Gault. Rock dust rolled at them and the rumbling sounds ceased. The cave stopped quivering. The dust settled and the two men spat. Then Garry lit a match and in the flame peered at the pile of rock debris. More than half of the length of the cave had fallen in.

'He's dead,' muttered Garry. 'Hell, did I kill him or was it rock? And the gold – it's buried.'

Ben Gault said, 'Thanks for the warning. You might have saved my life.'

'Who the hell are you?'

'Ben Gault, at your service.'

'I got your name long ago, *amigo*. I mean exactly who are you? What brought you here?'

'I trailed you.'

'Why? And why have you been snoopin' around?'

'Let's get to hell away from here,' said Ben Gault. 'More rock could fall, and I've got a thin skull . . .'

They climbed down to the base of the cliff face. Garry kept looking up. He could hardly believe that Caleb Kray was dead.

'Three had to die,' he muttered. 'They just had to die . . .'

Kray's two horses were tethered not far away and so was Ben Gault's mount. 'I saw the two animals,' said Gault, 'and I wondered. I guess I made a fool play showing myself in that cave mouth.'

'Why did you trail me?' Garry persisted.

'I'm a Pinkerton Detective Agency man, hired by the Powder River Mine. I've been on your trail since the day you left the Pen. I —'

'You're the jasper who cut me down from that hanging tree?'

'Yep. I didn't want you to know I was around, so I rode off when I saw you were alive. You see,

154

the recovery of the gold was my chief concern.'

Garry pointed to the cliff face. 'It's buried up there, what's left of it.'

'I knew it was there. I took a notebook from Kray's safe. and there was a drawing and a reference to the cave. I figured to retrieve the gold pretty soon, but events have beaten me to it.'

'I think you had suspicions all along about Kray and his pals.'

'Yes, when I saw you were so determined to kill them. And even before that, when they tried to hang you, I had hunches about them. But that wasn't proof. I told Hec Shield about you and that little fellow who called himself William Smith. I knew he'd been released from the Butte Pen and that he wasn't in town for fun.'

Garry Maine wiped rock dust from his face. He was suddenly bone-weary. 'It's over,' he said. 'They're dead. And the gold is buried.'

'Maybe the gold can be dug out – with the cave shored up. We'll see. Right now I suggest that we ride back, friend.'

Ben Gault was right; the gold was dug out and it was discovered that Kray had not died from a bullet wound. Falling rock had killed him, not Garry's shot. Hec Shield told Garry that he was free.

Garry went to the T Bar T that day. A girl was waiting for him. But she was in one of her bad moods. 'You could,' she rasped, 'get yourself dressed up! Throw away that damned sheepskin coat!'

Garry grinned at her. 'You can quit shouting, Lucia. We've got better things to do. For a start I ain't kissed you yet!'